BANK ROLL

A MAX STRYKER MYSTERY

BANK ROLL

A MAX STRYKER MYSTERY

By

Janet Elaine Smith

Other books by Janet Elaine Smith:

The Keith Trilogy: *Dunnottar, Marylebone, Par for the Course*

Patrick and Grace Mysteries: *In St. Patrick's Custody, Recipe for Murder, Old Habits Die Hard*

Women of the Week Series: *Monday Knight, Tuesday Nolan* (coming soon)

House Call to the Past
Pampas
Dakota Printer
And We'll Call Her General Leigh
My Dear Phebe
A Lumberjack Christmas
A Christmas Dream

Bank Roll
©Janet Elaine Smith 2007

ALL RIGHTS RESERVED
No part of this book may be reproduced in any form, by photocopying or by any electronic or mechanical means, including information storage or retrieval systems, without permission in writing from both the copyright owner and the publisher of this book, except for the minimum words needed for review.

Bank Roll is a work of fiction. All incidents and dialogue, and all names and characters are products of the author's imagination and are not to be construed as real.

ISBN: 1-932993-78-9
ISBN 13: 978-1-932993-78-3
Library of Congress Number
LCCN: 2007927470

Cover Art by Shane D. Foster
Cover Design by Joyce Anthony and Star Publish LLC
Interior Design by Mystique Design

A Star Publish Book
http://starpublish.com
Nevada, USA and St. Croix USVI

Published in 2007 by Star Publish LLC
Printed in the United States of America

To all the people I have known and admired,
Laughed with (and sometimes at)
Who live in Small Town, USA,
Wherever it is.
And especially in memory of
Audrey Kinder, my old English teacher,
Who believed in my ability to write,
And who nominated me for the National Honor Society.
Last but not least, to Mike Jacobs,
Editor of the *Grand Forks Herald,*
Which also went on the "auction block"
Because of the sale by Knight Ridder;
Keep on keeping on!

CHAPTER ONE

"Maggie!" the voice boomed as he charged into the house. "He's gone. Here, just look at this! He's been kidnapped, right before our very eyes. Can you believe it?"

Then the phone went dead. Max Stryker sat at her kitchen table, staring in disbelief at the phone in her hand. She had hung up on her! Her very own mother!

She had been through a lot in the last twenty-four hours. She twirled the *pink slip* around on the table. There was no point in arguing about it; everybody knew the St. Paul *Pioneer Press* might be nearing its last days. Knight Ridder had just announced that they had been bought out, and nothing was sure. But—she smiled—it was fun while it lasted.

She reread the notice in the latest trade magazine for the umpteenth time. *Wanted Immediately: reporter and editor to run successful small town newspaper. Owner/pub retiring.*

If only it was someplace else. She had tried so hard to get out of Willow Creek. It was so small there was no room for advancement in her future. Sure, old Joe McGrath had argued that she owed him everything she had; after all, he had taught her the newspaper business from one end to the other when she worked for him during her high school days. But that was then, and this was now.

"You've come a long way, baby!" she said, trying to convince herself of the truth of the statement. "You've been there and done it all. How could you even consider going back to your old stomping grounds once you've seen what big city life is like?"

She cringed at the mere thought of returning home. It was the one thing she had vowed she would never do. So many of her friends had been forced to return to their parents' homes because they couldn't make it in the outside world, but not Max. Oh, no! She was better than that. Her final words as she left Willow Creek were, "I'll show you!" as she looked in the rear view mirror and thumbed her nose—so adolescent-like—at the small-potato life she was leaving behind.

Now, about to do what she promised she would never do, she smiled as she thought of all the things she had learned from her father. Bud Stryker was the chief of police in Willow Creek. It didn't matter that he was the *only* cop in town. He was still the boss. Of course he was also the mayor, the head of the city council, and the president of the school board...

She punched the numbers on her phone automatically. *Funny,* she thought, *some things—like your own phone number—you never forget.* The busy signal growled angrily in her ear.

She dialed again, and again, and again, punching the redial button each time. Finally, her mother answered the phone. She had barely said "Hello" when Max heard her father bellow in the background.

"Keep that line clear, Ma! You know we have to have it open in case they find out where he's gone! Who'd a thunk it? A kidnapping!" And then the phone buzzed in Max's ear.

"Wonder who is missing?" she said aloud. Nothing exciting ever happened in Willow Creek. The biggest event she could ever remember was the time Pete Bjornson got run over by the moose. Poor old Pete! Neither Pete nor the moose survived that ordeal.

A kidnapping! That was about the most farfetched thing she'd ever heard of, at least in Willow Creek.

She punched the redial button again. Still busy. She kept redialing, time after time, hardly giving the line time to cool in between calls. Finally, she heard her mother answer again.

"Mother?" she asked. "What's going on up there? Did I hear Pops right? Somebody's been kidnapped?"

"That's right," her mother said.

"Is Pops on top of it already?" Max asked. Then, she knew what she had to do. He needed her. She had learned a lot while she was covering the crime beat on the big time St. Paul *Pioneer Press*. She had tracked down serial killers and kidnappers on an almost daily basis. She could certainly help Pops find a kidnapper in Willow Creek. After all, there were only 265 people there. No, she thought, 264; she had left. To her knowledge, no one had moved into town to take her place.

"I'm coming home," Max said. "Tell Joe I saw his ad. I'll be there in about four hours. He can't handle this by himself. It's too big for him."

A loud clap of thunder echoed through the phone and then it went dead. Max laughed. *Just like on TV,* she thought. *Every time something weird happens, it is in the middle of a storm.*

Max scurried around her apartment, shoving her belongings into suitcases. When they were full, she ran down to the basement to grab whatever boxes she could find.

****

Max's sleek white Jaguar slithered along the Interstate. Her mind seemed to be traveling faster than the car. She hated to admit defeat. This way, if there really was a kidnapping, it offered the perfect excuse. She didn't have to take out an ad, notifying everybody that she'd been sacked.

It was of little consolation, as she mulled the circumstances over and over, that it was the newspaper that failed—not her. Nobody ever imagined that the *Pioneer Press* wouldn't survive. Oh, sure, it might be bought up by somebody else, but it would never be the same. She was jobless, and she needed them. But, she was in control of this whole mess. She lifted her head heavenward, saying a silent "Thank you" to whoever was responsible for kidnapping the victim. It was exactly what she needed to save face back home in Willow Creek.

****

At the *Herald* office in Willow Creek, Joe McGrath rubbed his hands together in glee at the prospect of such a big story for his weekly edition. The sweat was pouring off his bald head. "It's the biggest news to hit town since the moose got loose and killed poor old Pete!" he said gleefully just as Mrs. Stryker walked in.

"Joe?" she asked, staring at him with concern. "You look like you're burning up with a fever! It's a good thing Maxine's coming home to rescue you."

"The only fever I've got is to get this type set and the paper run off. Shoot! If Rick and I can get it done on time, we might even come out with a special edition. Two papers in one week! Can you imagine that?"

Mrs. Stryker sensed that he was so excited he hadn't heard one word she had said about Maxine. Maybe this wasn't the time for such news, but it was obvious that he needed help. She never really did figure Rick was all that competent. He certainly couldn't take Maxine's place. Nobody could.

"So you heard the big news?" Mrs. Stryker asked.

"Of course," Joe said. "I should have known you'd have heard, too. I suppose Bud filled you in on all the details. Good, sit down." He grabbed a notepad and began to scribble. "Give me what you've got."

Mrs. Stryker wasn't about to admit—to Joe McGrath or anybody else—that the only thing Bud had told her was that the kidnappee was Bill Crane, the bank president. Any details disappeared with Bud when he raced out of the house as fast as he'd come into it.

"It's Bill Crane, over at the bank," she said.

"I know that!" Joe sputtered. "He's disappeared. There's no sign of him anywhere. His car is at the bank, but he never went home last night. When Sally got to the bank this morning she found it unlocked, so she figured he was already there. Working early. He did that a lot, you know."

"Yeah," Mrs. Stryker mumbled. "That and a whole lot more." She had learned more from Joe in the last two minutes than she knew, even if she was married to the chief of police and the mayor.

"Beg your pardon, Maggie. What'd you say?"

"Nothing," she answered. "Nothing important."

There wasn't any need for her to repeat it. Everybody in town knew his reputation with the girls at the bank. They all made sure they left well ahead of him, and as far as they all knew, he'd never been successful in seducing any of them, but it sure wasn't because he didn't try! *Yeah, this leaves a whole bevy of suspects*, she thought. There probably wasn't one single person in town—or married either, for that matter—who would be upset by Bill Crane's disappearance. Every woman, every husband, every father—they all hated him with a passion. A passion capable of—kidnapping? Sure, easy. Maybe even murder.

"I told him some day he'd get his come-uppance," Mrs. Stryker said. "So where'd he go?"

"Don't rightly know," Joe said, "but there was a ransom note on his desk. Asked for fifty thousand dollars. Can you fathom that? Old Bill, he thought he was priceless! Why, in a big city they'd have asked for a few million for a bank president. Guess he wasn't as valuable as he thought."

Joe laughed at the irony of the situation. He knew it was nasty, but he was almost glad somebody had tried to play games with Bill Crane. He remembered the time his own daughter had come home and told him about Bill's advances. He was ready to do a whole lot more than kidnap the guy. If Chief Stryker hadn't been there when he got to the bank, Joe would probably have killed him with his own bare hands.

"Sure wish Max was here to help me!" he grumbled as he kept on working at the typesetting machine. "Rick!" he hollered. "Can't depend on that kid for anything!"

Confirming Mrs. Stryker's suspicion that he hadn't heard a word she said, she repeated the information. "That's why I came over here in the first place. Maxine just called. She's coming home. She said she heard you were ready to retire and figured you needed some help. You know, somebody you could depend on."

"Figured the old man couldn't handle it any more, did she?" he said, trying to sound like he was complaining. Mrs. Stryker, however, saw the twinkle in his eye that Maxine had always put there. They had been a good team. It would be good to see them together again.

"Rick!" Joe yelled again.

"Yeah, boss?" the young man said as he nonchalantly wandered in through the back door with a can of soda pop in his hand.

"Where'd you go? We've got work to do! Important work!"

"Got thirsty," Rick replied, shrugging his shoulders.

Joe buried his head in his hands.

"Hurry home, Max," he said softly as Mrs. Stryker walked out the door.

CHAPTER TWO

Max's head was spinning by the time she pulled her car into a parking space in front of the *Herald* office. Would they believe her when she told them that she was coming home for their sake, not hers? Maybe she should have called Joe first, just in case he considered her a traitor. After all, he had accused her of jumping ship when she left for the big city. Or was it her own pride that stood in her way? She was here, despite her promises to never darken this door again. But, she reminded herself, she had learned a lot and they could certainly use her smarts now, with a kidnapping case on their hands.

She wondered again who it was that was missing. She should have checked her cell phone before she left St. Paul so she could have kept calling her mother back to find out, but the batteries were as dead as her big-time crime career.

Bolstering as much courage as she could, she opened the car door and slowly slid out. She had carefully chosen a very professional navy and white pinstriped suit and navy high heeled pumps for this important visit, hoping to make at least some sort of statement that she wasn't the same giddy girl who used to work here, clad in her Levi's and sweatshirt.

She carefully opened the door, remembering how it had always squeaked. She looked around, then froze. Who was this stranger sitting in Joe's place at the editorial desk? Had Joe died? She had not bothered to look at the date on the trade magazine she had seen his ad in. No, surely her mother would have told her if something had happened to Joe. But, he must have found a replacement. So, she wasn't needed here, either. No more than she was needed at a nonexistent newspaper in St. Paul.

She was tempted to turn around and walk out, but she didn't know where to go. She had decided, on her way to Willow Creek, that she wasn't going to live with her parents. She would find an apartment of her own as soon as she could.

The blond wonder at the computer terminal kept working, completely oblivious to her presence. *He looks like some Norse god,* Max thought, *with just a wisp of unruly hair hanging over his eyes.* He brushed at it periodically, but to no avail. As soon as his hand was withdrawn, it fell back again. His eyes burned a brilliant blue as they stared at the computer screen.

He must have bought the newspaper out from Joe, Max reasoned. Joe had fought computerization as long as she could remember. He would never stand for it now. Nobody changed that much, certainly nobody as stubborn as old Joe McGrath.

She was so enraptured by the stranger that she didn't hear the footsteps behind her.

"Mornin', ma'am," came Joe's familiar drawl. "Can I help you with somethin'?"

Max turned to face Joe. A look of shock registered when he saw who it was.

"What in tarnation are you doin' here?" he asked.

"I came because of this," she said, shoving the ad from the trade magazine into his hand. "I—I thought you needed me." She hesitated several moments, then added, "I guess I was wrong."

Max was staring at the man at the desk.

"Him?" Joe asked, laughing. "Why, that's just Rick. Guess they moved in here after you left. His dad bought out Ben's sawmill when he retired. You knew about that, didn't you?"

Max struggled with her memory. Her mother had sent her every issue of the *Herald*, but she always tossed it in a corner, unread. Now she wished she had at least scanned them.

"Oh, yeah," Max said softly. "Everybody knew that."

Well, at least maybe she still had a shot at the job. Something told her she should have paid more attention to what was going on in Willow Creek, just in case. Besides, if there really was a kidnapping, they weren't equipped to handle it without her.

"Rick," Joe called out, "got a minute? There's somebody here you ought to get to know."

Rick punched several buttons on the computer to store what he was working on, then got up and ambled over to Joe and Max.

"So you're Max?" he asked.

Max flipped their conversation over in her mind quickly, trying to remember if Joe had called her by name. No, she was sure he hadn't. Then how did this guy who was invading her territory identify her so easily?

"Always have been," she replied glibly, trying not to sound as irritated as she felt. "And you're Rick."

"Yup," he said, although it had not been a question. "Rick Brown. Sure glad you're back. I can handle the typesetting and all the computer stuff, but when it comes to layout and going out to get a story, I'm afraid I'm no match for you."

His smile, which stretched from ear to ear, warmed Max's heart and she realized she couldn't stay mad at this guy for very long. She wondered if it would stay that way, or if petty jealousy would end up getting in the way of what might be a beautiful relationship. Or, maybe even better, now that she was here, Joe could just send him packing to help his dad at the sawmill. He looked like he belonged there, anyway. He was definitely the outdoor type. He probably enjoyed hunting and fishing and trekking in the woods. She couldn't imagine him wanting to be cooped up in an office day in and day out. And she sure didn't need him dogging her as she went about her business.

"This couldn't be better," Joe said, taking Max's hand in his. "You must have smelled a story. Boy, have we got a dandy!"

"The kidnapping?" Max asked. "Mother told me, but she didn't say who it was. You mean it's for real?"

On the way back to Willow Creek she had convinced herself that it was really a joke someone was playing. Who could the victim be in Willow Creek, where everybody knew everybody?

"Yup," Joe said, grinning at the prospect of Max digging her teeth into a real story for a change. She had always been a top-notch reporter, and he suspected she was even better now, after spending time in the big city and learning the ropes from the real pros. "We got us a real-live kidnapping. Honest!"

Max blinked. "You're teasing me again, aren't you?" she asked Joe, watching his face for that twinkle he always got in his eye that was a dead giveaway for his playing games. When she couldn't find it, she said, "What some people won't do for a good story!"

"It really is," Rick said, taking her by the hand and pulling her towards the computer.

Max hurried to pull her hand away. She didn't need anybody to lead her around this office. She knew it better than anyone else—except Joe, of course.

Rick sat down in front of the terminal and turned it on. He recalled the information he had been working on and sat silently while Max read the copy on the screen.

It was all there. "Bill Crane, President of Willow Creek State Bank, Kidnapped," the headlines read.

Max skimmed through the copy, shaking her head in disbelief. Nothing like this had ever happened in Willow Creek before.

"Who did it?" Max asked.

"Don't know," Joe said. "That's your daddy's department. We just report the facts as we get them."

"I'd better get over there and see what's going on," she said, heading towards the door. She turned back and looked at Rick. "You coming along?"

"That's not my bag," he said. "Besides, now that you're back, I expect I'll be moving on."

"Now just a doggoned minute," Joe said. "It took two of us to run this place when you were here before. You might be good, little lady, but even you aren't that good. You can use Rick's help. He's mighty good with that machine over there. Hell, that's the only way I could get him to agree to work here was to buy that dang thing. Well, I got it, and he's sure enough going to stick around here and run it."

"In that case," Max said, "you'd better get a hustle on. If I know my dad, he won't be sitting around the office trying to figure things out. No, sir, he'll be out there trying to dig up the facts. We don't want to miss him."

"Aye, aye, captain!" Rick quipped as he gave Max a sharp military salute.

Max jumped into her car, unlocking the passenger door and waiting for Rick to get in. He waved at her as he jogged ahead towards the city arena, where one small office provided the quarters for the Willow Creek Police Department.

Her blood boiling again, she squealed the tires of her fancy car and pulled out into the nearly empty street. It was still fairly early, which might explain the lack of activity, but truth be told, this was just about as busy as Willow Creek ever got. Oh, except during the Wild Rice Festival, that is. Then life really happened.

It was only two blocks to the police station from the paper, but she was pleased that she got there before Rick. She had just gotten out of the car and locked the doors—a habit she had gotten into in the Twin Cities—when he ran up behind her.

"Ready?" he asked. Max noticed that he wasn't even breathing hard. Granted, it wasn't far to go, but she knew she would have been out of breath if she had run it.

"Let's go," she said, sounding irritated with his ever-presence.

Max pushed the door of her dad's office open with a bang, causing him to jump slightly at the noise.

"Max!" he said in surprise. "You're home?"

"Didn't Mom tell you I was coming?"

"Sure," he said, "but she didn't say when. Did you just get here?"

He went to his daughter and embraced her warmly. All of a sudden, he was aware that Rick was there, too.

"Did you meet him on your way in?" he asked.

"No," Max said. "He was over at the *Herald* when I went there this morning."

"Can't figure out why Maggie didn't tell me you'd hit town," he said.

"Guess I forgot to call her," Max admitted. "Can I use the phone?"

"Yeah, but she's gonna be mad that you didn't go there first. When did you get in?"

"About half an hour ago," Max said. She hesitated, then said, "I'm going to check in at the motel until I can find an apartment."

"Oh, well," he said, shrugging his shoulders and thinking that he would never understand the younger generation. Her room at home was still empty.

"I've really got to get back to work. This whole mess with Bill woke me up early this morning. Go ahead and make your call."

Rick felt like he was watching a TV crime show. Bud Stryker acted just like he was giving a criminal his one allowable phone call to his attorney.

Max was pleasant to her mother, but told her that she had work to do. "I'll see you for supper," she said, hanging the phone up and turning back to her dad.

"So it is true," Max said, still not able to comprehend such a thing happening in Willow Creek. "How'd it happen?"

"Don't know a whole lot about it yet," Bud said. "Sally found the note when she went to work this morning."

"Sally? Sally Kant?" Max threw her head back and laughed. "Everybody always said there was nothing Sally Can't do. Well, wouldn't you know it? If somebody's going to be in the middle of a mess like this, of course it would be Sally."

"You think she staged the whole thing?" Bud asked Max. "I heard different times that Bill was sweet on the kid."

"Bill sweet on Sally? Pops, you know as well as I do that there isn't a girl in this town Bill Crane hasn't tried to hit on. Only thing is, he's got such a big belly on him and his legs are so short he can't run as fast as any of them. That's the only thing that ever made it safe for any woman to work at the bank. Everybody hated Bill Crane!"

"I hate to cut you off, but I really do have to get back to work on this. It's not every day I have a case like this to figure out."

"It's not every day you have a parking ticket to issue!" Max joked. "We'll get busy and see what we can find out."

"Just a minute here, young lady," he said, grabbing her by the arm and spinning her around to face him. "We don't know what we're dealing with. Granted, this is a sleepy little town, but all kinds of weird things happen anymore. Ain't nobody safe. Now, I don't want you messin' in this. I promise as soon as I find out anything, I'll pass the information on to you. But this is a job for a cop, not some know-it-all reporter that thinks she can do anything just because she's been trained in some fancy city."

"Sure, Pops," Max said, walking out the door.

"You coming?" she called out to Rick as she got into her car.

This time he got in, unsure of what she was up to, but knowing instinctively that she wasn't going to pay any attention to her father's warning.

"Where we headed?" he asked.

"To the bank," Max answered. "We've got to talk to Sally. After all, she knows as much of the story as anybody. If we want the truth, we'd better talk to her before Dad questions her. Sure as anything he'll tell her not to give us anything."

"You don't think he's already talked to her?" Rick asked.

"Not likely," Max said. "He doesn't move as fast as he used to."

The car glided smoothly up to the curb in front of the bank. Curiosity had obviously gotten the best of everybody, as it was probably the biggest crowd they had ever had.

"Come on," she ordered Rick. "We've got a story to cover." *And a mystery to solve,* she thought, rubbing her hands together at the prospect.

CHAPTER THREE

Max hurried into the bank, pushing her way past the people she had known all her life, but who were suddenly a blur of unimportant faces.

"Where's Sally?" she asked no one in particular.

"Over there," Mary Bertheson answered. Then she turned to Gerry LaPlant. "Isn't that Max?" she asked. "When did she blow into town?"

"Beats me," Mary said, "but you might know if there's trouble afoot Max isn't far behind."

"You think she..." Karyn Ingersoll asked, then shook her head in disbelief. "She'd never kidnap..."

"Remember Mrs. Kindred's dog?" Mary reminded her cohorts at the bank.

They all nodded in agreement. They would never forget the time Mrs. Kindred gave Max a D on an English paper, and Max stole her dog, Perkins, for revenge. But this was different. This was Bill Crane, not a helpless mutt.

"Do you suppose he...you know...came after her, too?"

"Naw," Gerry said. "Besides, she never worked at the bank. She was always too busy with old Joe at the paper."

"That never stopped Bill," Karyn said. "You know what he did to Beth Hatcher."

"Or tried to," Mary said. The girls all laughed. "And she was a married woman. I'll bet Hank never knew she could kick that high!"

They all laughed again. Everybody in town had heard where Beth kicked Bill. He walked with a slight stoop for days afterwards.

****

"Sally!" Max called out as she walked to Bill's office.

Sally Kant had always been the coolest, most in-control person anyone ever knew. *Nothing* phased Sally! Now, as Max studied her sitting behind Bill's big impersonal desk, she was stunned. She was actually crying!

"Sally! It's me, Max. Don't you worry about anything. We'll fix this. You know us; between you and me, kid, we can figure this thing out."

"You don't understand," Sally said between her sobs. "Your dad just called. He's coming over to question me."

"That's just standard procedure," Max said, trying to sound reassuring. "I'm sure he just wants to ask you about the note you found."

"How'd you know about the note?" Sally asked, fear shining through the tears in her big, deep brown eyes. "I didn't tell anybody about it."

"Except Pops," Max explained. "He told me. When I was in St. Paul I covered the cop beat, you know. I'm going to give Pops a hand on this one."

The two friends of the past were interrupted by two voices--in unison--asking, "You're going to *what*?"

Max hadn't seen either Rick or her father follow her into the office. If she had, she probably wouldn't have been quite so bold in her declaration.

"I just mean, I will keep my eyes and ears open," she said, trying to quickly pass over the issue to something else.

"I told you to keep out of this!" Bud warned sternly. "We don't know what we're dealing with. It could be dangerous."

"I don't know anybody in Willow Creek I'd classify as dangerous," Max said, chuckling, "except maybe Paul Bunyan."

Bud glared at Max, trying desperately to catch her eye. He had never been particularly fond of Paul Bunyan. Or of Sally, for that matter, but he sure didn't want to cross him. No, he was a force to be reckoned with, and he had to find a way to warn Max not to step on his toes.

John Martin—that was his real name—but everybody called him Paul Bunyan. Never *Paul*, always *Paul Bunyan*--and with good reason. He was a lumberjack, but he was also about the same dimension as Paul Bunyan. At least he was as close to it as was apt to exist.

Bud was sure Maggie had written to Max about Paul Bunyan and Sally getting married. It was the strangest wedding the town had ever seen. Sally wore a micro-mini skirt--white, of course--with a white-fringed leather jacket and a veil. Paul Bunyan wore his traditional blue jeans, his size 19 logger's boots and his red and black buffalo plaid shirt. Sally's attendants, her friends from the bank, each wore a long formal gown in red velvet. After all, it was a Christmas wedding! The men who stood up for Paul Bunyan wore black tuxedos—and plaid flannel shirts! Even if Maggie hadn't told Max about it, Bud knew she always sent the weekly papers to her, and surely she wouldn't have missed that. There was even a front-page picture of the happy couple.

"Sally," Bud asked, hoping to shut Max up before she did or said something really stupid, "was Paul Bunyan home last night?"

"Sure," Sally answered. "Why?"

"Just checking," Bud said, trying to sound calm. "In a little town like this everybody's a suspect until we rule them out. What about this morning? Early."

"He left for the woods, just like he always does, by six o'clock," Sally said. "He went right to work."

Bud took his little black book out of his inside jacket pocket and wrote something in it.

"You don't think Paul Bunyan..." Sally asked, her voice drifting off into the unfinished question.

"Don't know," Bud said. "Like I said, we just have to check on everybody. I'm sure the FBI will have more questions for both of you when they get here. You especially."

"Why me?" Sally asked, her hands shaking nervously.

"Well, you did find the note," Bud said.

"Oh, yeah, sure. I s'pose that's why."

Max grabbed Bud by the arm and pulled him off to the side, Rick close at their heels.

"What do you mean, the FBI?" she asked. "We can certainly figure out whodunit. Why would we need them? These people won't talk to them. They'll clam up like crazy. They trust us. We can do a lot more."

"*We* won't do anything!" Bud said emphatically. "I told you, Max, stay out of this one! It's too big for you. It's too big for me. And it's sure too big for Farmer Brown here! Besides, you know kidnapping is a federal crime. I didn't have any choice in the matter. I had to call them in on it."

"I suppose so," Max said, shrugging her shoulders and turning to walk away. Bud put his hand on her shoulder to stop her.

"Another thing," he said, his voice sounding a warning, "have you forgotten about Sally and Paul Bunyan? Anything you say against him to Sally is sure to get back to him."

"Why?" Max asked, a puzzled look crossing her face.

"You didn't know they got hitched?" Rick asked. "It was in the paper."

"Sally and Paul Bunyan? Married?" Max exclaimed. "No!"

"Yup," Bud said, "so you'd best watch your step with her. Funny, but she's as protective of him as he is of her."

"But he's old enough to be her father!" Max protested.

"You've never heard that love is blind?" Rick asked.

"Dumb, too!" Bud grumbled. "Those two prove it."

"Now, I've told you before and I won't tell you again, go on over to the paper office and do your job. Leave the crime fighting to me. To *us*," he corrected himself, remembering that for the first time in his life he would have outside help on a case. He'd never needed outside help before. Shoot, he hardly ever had a case before.

"Sure, Pops," Max said. She turned and winked teasingly at Rick. "You ready, Rick? We'd better get back to work. We do have a paper to put out, you know."

"Coming," Rick said, following along behind her.

"Congratulations!" Max said as she passed by Sally, still sitting with her head in her hands at Bill's desk. "I heard you got married."

"Thanks," Sally said, not really hearing what Max had even said. No, she didn't have time to dwell on unimportant issues. If Bud Stryker thought Paul Bunyan might be involved in this, it was a pretty safe bet the FBI men would come to the same conclusion. Especially if they found out Bill had gone to visit Sally when he heard Paul Bunyan was stuck out in the woods and wouldn't be back that night. How were they supposed to know Paul Bunyan could physically pick up the end of the truck and get it out of the mud and would find his way home? Yes, she had her work cut out for her. Somehow, she had to keep them all from finding out about it.

****

Sally reached for the Rolladex on Bill's desk. She knew the number for the banking commissioner in St. Paul was in there. Maybe, if she reported the kidnapping to the powers-that-be before anybody else, it would help make her and Paul Bunyan look less guilty. She knew Paul Bunyan wouldn't kill anyone. She knew a side of him—a softer, gentler side—that few people ever saw.

"I'll get somebody on it right away," the commissioner said. "I'll send someone up there to cover it until they find out what's happened to Bill. Oh, and thank you for calling, Miss Kant. I'll see that it goes on your record."

"Thank you, sir," Sally said, replacing the receiver on the cradle.

"What's that all about?" Tom Garborg asked the commissioner. "Trouble?"

"Seems so," the commissioner replied. "Looks like old Bill Crane's gone and gotten himself kidnapped."

Tom leaned back and howled hysterically.

"Something I said?" the commissioner asked.

"No," Tom said, talking between laughs. "It's just that it's about time somebody got the old goat. Mind if I go up there and take over? You said you had to send somebody. Why not me?"

"What's in it for you?" the commissioner asked.

"A guy can't try to help out?" Tom asked.

"It's not exactly your nature," the commissioner said, "but I guess it might as well be you as somebody else. You've got it."

Tom smiled. He'd have to figure out what to tell Carol. Good thing she was pregnant again. That gave him the perfect excuse for her to stay in the Twin Cities. He would come back on weekends, of course. Oh, yeah, this was perfect. If they never found Bill Crane it would be too soon for him.

****

Max got into her Jag and waited for Rick to join her. Instead, he began walking towards the *Herald* office.

"Get in!" Max ordered.

"I'd rather walk," he said.

"I said, 'Get in!' We've got to talk. We can't do it in front of Joe. He'll get all worried. He's like an old mother hen, you know. Worries about everything."

Rick got in, mumbling something under his breath.

"What'd you say?" Max asked.

"Nothing," he said. He wasn't about to admit that he had just said that it was quite obvious that with Max around, Bud had plenty of reason to be worried. He was worried about her, too, and he'd just met her.

He glanced at his watch. "Unbelievable!" he said.

"What is?" Max asked.

"Do you realize that we have only known each other for two hours, and already you are driving me crazy? Are you going to do what your father said and stay out of this whole crazy mess?"

He knew the answer before she said a word. He also knew she wouldn't level with him about it.

To his surprise, she said, quite openly and truthfully, "Not on your life, man! Not for a minute!"

"You don't get it, do you?" Rick asked, shaking his head so that one chunk of hair bobbed around in front of his eyes. "You think you've got a job to do, and nothing or nobody is going to stop you from it. Have I got it right?"

"Almost," Max said, grinning at him. "*We've* got a job to do and nobody is going to stop *us!*"

Rick groaned, admitting defeat.

CHAPTER FOUR

"What have you been up to?" Joe asked when Max and Rick walked into the office at the *Herald*. "As if I didn't know."

"Nothing much," Max said.

"Rick?" Joe asked, knowing he'd never get the truth out of Max. She was like a pit bull when she got after something. She wouldn't let loose until she had her prey in her mouth.

"Just checking out the story," Rick said.

Max breathed a sigh of relief. So she could count on Rick after all. If he wasn't going to stick with her, he'd have ratted on her now. Maybe he wouldn't be so bad to work with. Besides, he had admitted that he didn't really know anything about the newspaper business—just computers. So, she had free rein to run the whole show. And Joe...well, she wouldn't have to worry about him. She could see that the arthritis in his hip was bothering him far more than it had when she'd left town. He was no threat. He couldn't keep up with her; he'd be lost in the dust if he tried.

"What's the big news on it?" Joe asked.

"Guess it's that Pop's called in the FBI," Max said, laughing. "Can you figure that one? The FBI right here in Willow Creek! I'll bet those guys will think they've hit Outer Slobovia when they get a look at this town."

"You mean when they land," Joe said, correcting Max. "They are coming in here by helicopter this afternoon. I want you both out at the old landing strip when they set that whirlybird down."

"The old landing strip?" Max asked in disbelief. "Nobody's used that in years. Not since Pete had that little two-seater he used to fly people in on for fishing. It's got to be grown over with weeds and everything else. They'll never even find it."

"Guess you can land one of those rigs most anyplace," Joe said. "That's what I hear, anyway. I've never been in one myself, but haven't you ever seen them on TV? Why, little girl, I reckon they could land on the roof right here at the *Herald* if they wanted to."

"And that would be the end of the roof on the *Herald*," Max scoffed. "It hardly holds the snow up, let alone a helicopter."

"Where's the landing strip?" Rick asked.

"Boy, you sure haven't had much of a life here, have you?" Max asked him. "You ever heard of Blueberry Hill?"

"Sure, Fat's Domino sang about it. Years ago."

"Doubt if it was this one," Joe said. "This one has the best darn blueberries this side of Canada. And right at the foot of Blueberry Hill is the old landing strip."

"I can't believe it," Max said, shaking her head. "You've really never heard of Blueberry Hill? How long have you lived here?"

"Almost two years," Rick replied.

"Maybe that's why," Max said. "You were too old when you got here. It's the local hangout for all the kids. You know, they go out there and make out. But then I guess you were past the high school crowd when you got to town."

"Afraid so," Rick said. "Maybe you can finish my education some night."

Max realized it was the first time she had seen him smile. His face lit up and he seemed even more handsome than before. That wisp of blonde hair in his eyes was suddenly incredibly sensuous.

She slapped her face slightly, hoping to bring herself back to reality.

"Sure, sometime. But for now we've got work to do."

She turned to face Joe. "Where can we find Paul Bunyan?"

"What do you want him for?" Joe asked.

"Not sure yet, but Pops hinted that he thinks he might be involved in Bill's disappearance somehow."

"Guess he's the one guy in town who could manage to haul him off—single-handedly. Last I heard he was cutting timber out on the old Parsons place. It's up for sale, you know. When Dan died, Wilma couldn't pay the taxes, so the county took it over. They hired Paul Bunyan to clear part of it, hoping it would bring a better price. All the news about a shortage of trees, they ought to take a look over there. Man, it's so thick you have to chop your way in."

"Let's go," Max said, grabbing Rick by the hand. It made him feel like a little boy again, and he wasn't sure if that was a good feeling or a bad one.

"Coming, Ma," he quipped. "Be back whenever," he said to Joe as they went out the door.

Joe started to say something, but Rick interrupted him. "I know, I know. We've got a paper to put out. I'll get the typesetting done, even if I have to stay up all night. If we don't stay on top of this story, nobody will, but the paper has to come out anyway."

"You sound like somebody else I know," Joe said, tipping his head in Max's direction.

They drove alone on the highway until they got to County Road H. Max swerved onto the gravel road and Rick dug his fingernails into the thickly padded dashboard.

"You're going to run us into the ditch!" he screamed. "Besides, you're going to scratch your pretty new car."

"What kind of car do you have?" Max asked.

"Nineteen-forty-two pickup," he said, beaming proudly. "Red."

"I should have known," Max said under her breath.

****

"Maggie," Bud Stryker said into the mouthpiece on his phone. "I won't be home for dinner. Probably not for supper, either."

"But Maxine's home. She's going to be here for supper. You can't disappoint her. She'll be anxious to see you."

"No problem," Bud said. "I've already seen her."

"I should have known," Maggie grumbled. "Like father like daughter. I suppose she's in over her head, too."

"She better not be!" Bud yelled. "I told her to stay out of this one. It's too dangerous."

Maggie gasped. Sure, Bud was a policeman when she married him, but nothing in his job had ever been dangerous. Not until now. She wasn't prepared for this. She wasn't sure she could handle it. Not at all.

"So Bill really was kidnapped?" she asked.

"So it seems," Bud said. "Don't know much yet, but I've got the ransom note here in front of me. I'm trying to make some sense out of it."

"What's it say?" Maggie asked.

"He's put the move on one of us for the last time," Bud read. "He's safely hidden away. Leave $50,000 in unmarked bills in the dumpster out behind the bank. Don't try anything funny. Then tell all the women he's ever hurt that they'll all get their share of the ransom. It will probably end up to be less than $500. apiece, which is little reward for all he's put them through over the years. When he's good and tired of sharing his own company, I'll let him go--unharmed. Any funny business and I can't be responsible for what I might be forced to do."

"Did the writer sign it?" Maggie asked.

"That's the dumbest thing you've ever said!" Bud said. "I don't know why I even bother talking to you. I shouldn't anyway, you know. You're not a cop. This should be kept strictly confidential. Whoever heard of a kidnapper signing his own name to a ransom note?"

"Have you talked to Mrs. Kindred about the note?" Maggie asked.

"Why would I want to do that?" Bud asked.

"Now who's dumb?" Maggie snapped at him. "There's not a person in this town she hasn't taught English to. She might recognize the writing."

"The note was typewritten," Bud said matter-of-factly. "Hard to tell handwriting from that."

"I don't mean the handwriting," Maggie explained. "I mean the style of writing. She knows how everybody in town says everything. Something about the way it's worded just might give her a clue."

There was a silence on the line. Finally he said, "I don't have any other clues. I suppose it's worth a shot. See you whenever I can."

The phone went dead in Maggie's ear. It was no different than any other phone conversation they'd ever had, but no matter how long she lived with Bud Stryker, she would never get used to it.

"Sure wish you'd learn to say 'goodbye!'" she complained. It was such a small issue, but it really irked her.

****

"Bud," Mrs. Kindred said as she stood in the doorway at her home. "Come on in. Surely you don't think I kidnapped Bill Crane!"

"The thought hadn't even crossed my mind. You didn't, did you?"

Mrs. Kindred faked a shocked, horrified look at the mere suggestion.

"No, sir. You can cross me off your list of suspects. I have an airtight alibi. I had to take Sam to the hospital last night. He was sure he was having an attack of appendicitis, or at the very least a gall bladder attack. I was there all night long."

"I'm sorry," Bud said. "Is Sam okay?"

"Yes, he's fine. Or at least he will be once he recovers from eating an entire pizza, fried oysters and a quart of rum cherry ice cream."

"Ych!" Bud said, contorting his face into an unbelievable shape at the idea of such a combination. "He ate that?" Bud asked. "All at once?"

"Well, within about an hour. When Doc Blank asked him why on earth he ate that stuff, he said 'Because I was hungry!' It surprises me he survived."

"Anyway, news travels fast. You've obviously heard about Bill."

"Yes," Mrs. Kindred said. "I'm sure by now everyone has. It doesn't take long for news that big to get all the way across town."

"Yeah," Bud said. "All six blocks of it. So you are playing hooky? I went to the school first, looking for you. Blanch said you'd called in sick."

"I swear, they need a new secretary at the school. Blanch can't hear anything straight any more. I told her, plain as day, that *Sam* was sick."

"Now, getting back to Bill," she said, "what do you want from me? I didn't kidnap him. I couldn't have dragged him off by myself. Why, my heels would have broken under the sheer weight of the oaf."

Bud looked down at her shoes. She was right, of course. No one in Willow Creek had ever seen Mrs. Kindred without her three-plus-inch high heels on. Maybe not even Sam, Bud laughed silently. He wondered if she slept in them.

"Besides," Mrs. Kindred continued, "if it had been up to me, I would have killed him. No, kidnapping is too good for him. Not for all he's done to the women in this town."

"Or tried to do," Bud said, wondering if Bill Crane had ever scored with any of the women. Even his wife!

"What I really need is for you to look at the ransom note," Bud said, handing the note to her.

She started to take it out of the Ziploc bag he had put it in to preserve any fingerprints until the FBI men got there. He didn't have any facilities for fingerprinting. The only time he could remember when he might have benefited from it was when the kids tipped over old Pete Miller's outhouse on Halloween. Yeah, he could have found out who the kids were that time, but he had a feeling he would have caught his own daughter, as well as half the other kids in town.

"Stop!" Bud yelled. "Leave it in the bag! There might be prints on it."

"What do you want me to do with it?" she asked, reading it over silently.

"Any guesses as to who might have written it?" Bud asked.

"I don't recognize the typing!" she said sarcastically.

"No," Bud said. "Does the style of writing or the way it's worded say anything to you?"

She studied it carefully for several minutes. "I'm not sure. I'd have to get out some old papers and compare them. Can you leave it here?"

"No," he said. "It's evidence. I have to keep it locked up. It's the only clue we've got right now. I'll make a copy and send it over to you. Take your time. Sounds like he's safe. I don't think we are looking for a murderer. Just revenge."

"It's about time," Mrs. Kindred said, and Bud had to admit he really didn't disagree with her, but he had his job to do, no matter how low the scum was that had been kidnapped.

"I've got to get going," Bud said. "We've got the FBI coming in pretty soon. I don't want them to think I'm not on the job. I left the office unattended."

Mrs. Kindred smiled. As long as she had lived in Willow Creek, nobody except Bud Stryker had ever been at the police office. If Bud wasn't there, it was always unattended.

"Tell Sam I hope he's feeling better," Bud said on his way out.

"Serve him right if his stomach hurt for a week!" she said.

She was mad at Sam. That was as clear as the nose on your face. Most women would yell at their husbands if they did such a stupid trick. Not Mrs. Kindred. For the first time in her life, Bud figured, she had just said an incomplete sentence! Yes, she was definitely mad! *Mad enough to kidnap somebody?* he wondered idly. She said she didn't have any part in it. Could he believe her? Could he believe anybody? Well, her alibi was easy enough to check out.

****

"I'm sure I won't be gone long," Tom Garborg told his wife, Carol, as she meticulously folded a shirt to pack in his suitcase. "I mean, how hard can it be to catch a crook in Willow Creek? A week would be more than enough to follow everybody in town!"

"You're doing it again," Carol said, cramming the red and white striped can of Barbasol shaving cream on top of his shirt, carefully squirting one little smidgeon onto it. "You always make fun of my hometown. I can't help it that I'm such a hick."

"I'm sorry," he said, walking over behind her and rubbing her shoulders. "I don't mean to. You know I love you more than anything in the world. And you aren't a *hick*; you're the classiest dame I ever met." He turned her around and kissed her, straining to get over her so-pregnant belly.

"I can't figure it out," she said. "Why would anybody want to kidnap old Bill Crane? Kill him—that I could understand—but kidnapping? It doesn't make any sense."

"So, you know all the local yokels," Tom said. "Who would be your prime suspect?"

Carol scratched her head. "Well, there's...and...and..." She groaned as the baby gave her a good swift kick. "I don't know. If I was married to that oaf, I'd have knocked him off years ago. There is nothing worse than a woman spurned. And Bill Crane certainly spurned his wife—time after time after time. If it was anybody, I'd lay odds on her. But, I don't think she'd have the smarts to figure out such a plot. No, it could be almost anybody."

"Good thing we were both here," Tom said. "They might think we were in on it."

"Maybe it's a multiple deal," Carol said, laughing. "I'll bet they all got together and dragged him out to the woods someplace and tied him to a tree. There's only one thing I regret."

"Do I dare ask?" Tom inquired, raising his big bushy eyebrows.

"Sure," she said. "It's simple. That they didn't count me in."

CHAPTER FIVE

Max sat at the composition desk, the light glaring up at her from the glass top. She sorted the various items, trying to fit them into their proper columns for the next edition of the *Herald*.

"Hey!" Rick said, holding another page he had just finished typesetting on the computer out to her. "Where are you?"

"Stupid question!" Max barked at him. "You can see I am right here."

"In body, maybe," he said, "but not in spirit."

"Just keep on working," Max said. She had always prided herself on being a realist. She didn't have time for daydreamers. Now, she found it hard to concentrate on the menial tasks that lay before her. She wished she was out on her cop beat in St. Paul. Or even out digging up the facts for this crisis in Willow Creek. If she could just sink her teeth into it, she was sure she could solve the case long before the FBI even got a good start. Then she would be the hero of the town.

"Boy," Rick said, smiling at her, "touchy, aren't we?"

"*We* are not!" she retorted.

"You just proved my point," Rick affirmed. "You are even touchy about being touchy."

"Will you get back to work?" Max asked, exasperated by his interruption.

"No," he said simply. No further explanation, just a sharp, clear, "No."

"And why not?" Max asked.

"We have to get to that landing strip. It's almost time for the FBI helicopter to come in. Remember, Joe asked us to meet it."

"Sure," Max said. "I still don't understand why Pops had to call them in here like some crazy army. He should have given us a chance to figure it out first. I mean, he could have done it himself, if he'd just set his mind to it."

"Jealous?" Rick asked, watching her reaction.

"Of some big feds? No way! Why would I be?"

"I know this sounds hopelessly impossible, but they just might do a better job of this than you would."

"Fat chance!" Max complained. "Still, I wish we'd had enough time to work on it some before they got here. Oh, what the heck, we should be able to dodge one smart-alecky t-man from Washington while we follow up the leads we come up with."

"Leads?" Rick asked. "What leads?"

"Weren't you listening?" Max asked. "How did you ever get to be a reporter anyway? You don't listen to a thing people say."

"Such as?" Rick asked.

"Didn't you hear Pops talking to Sally? He thinks she and Paul Bunyan are in on the kidnapping."

"I didn't hear him say that," Rick said, scratching his head, then brushing his flying cowlick back off his face.

"You listened to the words. You have to learn to listen to the silence, too."

"You don't make any sense at all," Rick said.

"When Pops asked Sally where Paul Bunyan was all night, that meant that he had some reason to suspect him. He is the one person in town who could have managed to haul Bill off. I mean, Bill is big. Fat. But Paul Bunyan, well, sure, he's big, but he's more than that. He's strong. Strong as an ox."

"Yeah," Rick quipped, "and his name is Babe. Anyway, if Paul Bunyan kidnapped Bill, why? He's never cared two cents about money. He works for the sheer joy of accomplishing something."

"You could be right. But there's Sally to consider, too."

"How does she fit into this whole thing? You think she is lying to protect him? But what about the ransom note?"

"What about it?" Max asked. "You know who discovered it."

"Sally," Rick said, beginning to see the light.

"OK," Max said. "Or so she said. It was still pretty early when she called Pops. And she was the only one at the bank. The note was typed, you know."

"So you're saying that Paul Bunyan went to the bank and carried Bill Crane out to his car. No, wait, he has a pickup. What did he do? Throw the body in the box to haul it off to who knows where while Sally went to the bank, typed a ransom note and then called your dad to come to the scene of the crime? The crime she and Paul Bunyan had just completed?"

"Something like that," Max said. "When I know she's going to be alone, I want to go over and talk to Sally. I have a feeling she knows a lot more than she's been willing to own up to."

"After we get the FBI guys," Rick said, going out the door and getting into his own pickup. "Ride with me?" he called out to Max.

"I guess so," Max said. "No sense in getting my car all scratched up. There's sure to be brambles and stuff out by Blueberry Hill."

Like a flash of lightening, she imagined a well-dressed FBI detective sliding into Rick's old beat-up pickup, perhaps spreading his white handkerchief on the seat so he wouldn't soil his crisp pin-striped suit pants. She grinned.

"Something funny?" Rick asked.

"No," she said, debating about whether or not to offer a dare as to if their unknown federal agent to try to fit in in a town the likes of Willow Creek. "Let's go."

She struggled to climb up into the pickup, her skirt too tight and her heels too high to offer her enough balance to mount the beast.

"Need a boost?" Rick asked, placing his hands around her waist and lifting her easily into the cab. Max felt the color rise in her face, but it seemed as natural as could be to Rick. She wondered how many other women he had lifted in to join him in a ride to... Well, she knew one thing. It wasn't to Blueberry Hill. He didn't even know the place existed until this morning.

"Thanks," Max managed to say. She didn't like the feeling of owing this near stranger anything, not even a free lift into his pickup. "Why do you have such big wheels on this rig, anyway?"

"It's better out in the woods," Rick explained. "When we first came up here, I was always getting hung up on some roots or a stupid tree trunk. This way I can sail right over the top of them."

Max realized that she didn't know much of anything about Rick or his family, except that they had moved in after she had left home and his dad ran the sawmill.

"Where'd you come from?" she asked. "I mean, where did you live before you moved here? And why did you come? I know Joe said your dad is running Ben's old sawmill."

"You're a little nosy, aren't you?" he asked.

Max wondered if she had overstepped the boundary lines he had set up against such questions. He fidgeted nervously with the steering wheel as they drove along.

"Take a right here," she instructed. "We're almost there."

She waited, wondering if he would answer her questions, or would he try to change the subject? Slowly, hesitantly, he began to speak.

"My dad was a high school teacher. He taught industrial tech. You know, shop and stuff like that. He always loved working with wood and with his hands. When he saw the ad that the sawmill here was for sale, he couldn't resist. Besides, Mom had just died and he really needed to get away from everything that reminded him of her."

"I'm sorry," Max said. There really was a soft side to this man. She wanted to reach out and take hold of his hand that was thumping so hard on the crossbar of the steering wheel, but she didn't know how he would react. "I'm sorry" was the best she could muster.

"I was going to start college, but I didn't want Dad to be alone. I suppose by now you have guessed that I have sort of a love affair with computers. The things totally fascinate me. I wanted to major in computer programming and get a job someday making computer software. But, that had to go on hold. Maybe someday..."

His voice trailed off dreamily. Max didn't know why, but she was surprised to learn that he had dreams he had to vacate on the way to reality. To life. It wasn't fair.

"We have something in common, your dad and me," she said.

"What?" he asked, then grinned that big-dipper grin of his. "Besides me, I mean?"

Max again blushed. That wasn't at all what she meant, so she'd better explain in a hurry.

"Not you, silly. We both came here because of a newspaper ad."

"You?" Rick asked in surprise. "I thought you were born and raised here."

"Oh, I was. But when I left, I vowed I would never come back—except for a visit once in awhile. Then the *Press* was sold and I couldn't get on at the *Tribune*. Everybody was looking for work. I was getting pretty desperate. The rent was already late. Then somebody gave me a page from a trade paper. And there it was! Like it was meant to be. Do you believe in fate?"

She kept right on talking, not waiting for him to answer. "It was Joe's ad for somebody to take over at the *Herald*. It never entered my head that he might have somebody else working for him. I just figured I was God's great answer to his problem. Then I walked in, and there you were."

"You don't have to worry about me. I'm afraid Joe has been more than patient with me. Like I told you before, I don't really know anything about running a newspaper. Joe was trying to teach me, but I'm afraid I'm a pretty slow learner. He does need you."

"Where did your dad teach school?" Max asked, glad that he seemed to be opening up to her at least a little.

"Minneapolis, Roosevelt High," he answered.

"You used to live in Minneapolis?" Max asked, surprise registering in her voice.

"Why is that so shocking?"

"You just don't seem like the big city kind of guy," she said.

"Is that a compliment or an insult?" Rick asked.

"Compliment. Most of the guys I met in down there were so phony. So fickle."

Rick wondered if someone had broken her heart in the big city and that was at least part of her reason for coming home.

"So I've learned my lesson well?" he asked, winking at her. "I've lost all my city-slickerness?"

"I can't imagine you ever had any," she confessed. Afraid to open old wounds, but wanting more answers, she asked, "What happened to your mother? You said she died."

Rick's face turned an ashen white. He didn't want to talk about it. It still hurt too much. But, maybe if she knew the truth, maybe then she'd understand if he didn't get too gung-ho about this whole kidnapping deal.

"She was killed," he said, his face glued to the road directly in front of him like he was reliving whatever it was that was so painful. "In the line of duty."

"The line of duty?" Max asked. "Your mother was a cop?"

"Yup, just like your dad. Only difference is that it's a lot more dangerous in Minneapolis. But then you know that. You just came from there, and you covered the cop beat on your *investigative reporting*. Dad wanted Mom to give it all up a couple of years earlier, but she wouldn't hear of it. Finally, she agreed that when he retired she'd quit and they would move to some sleepy-hollow town where the biggest excitement that ever happened was an overdue traffic ticket." He hesitated a few moments, then added, "Dad was due to retire exactly one month from the day Mom was shot."

"I'm sorry," Max said again. It seemed so shallow. So inadequate. But if it made any difference, she meant it from the bottom of her heart.

She felt an urge to protect Rick from further hurt. Like he was a little boy. Suddenly, she knew how Sally felt about Paul Bunyan.

"Well, you found your Paradise," Max said, hoping she would find the right thing to say. She could sense his uneasiness at discussing things so close to his heart.

"I thought so," Rick said. "Until today, that is. Now maybe you can understand why I can't get so hepped up over this kidnapping. I've seen more than my share of heartache and turmoil—with Mom in her job. I know if Dad finds out I'm involved in this mess, he'll be mad as hell."

"Look!" Max exclaimed, pointing to the helicopter overhead. "How's that for timing? Pull in there. That's Blueberry Hill just up ahead. Wow! I never thought I'd see a helicopter—or FBI men—in Willow Creek!"

"And I thought I'd get a chance to investigate what makes Blueberry Hill so special before they got here," Rick teased.

****

Tom Garborg's car was headed straight north. His goal was as set as the compass needle on his dashboard. It was sure a good thing Carol was too close to her due date to argue about going along. No, this sounded like a real mess up in Willow Creek. He knew one thing. He had to keep a close eye on what developed. He heard Carol's words echoing in his ears over and over as he drove. "If he was my husband, I'd do more than kidnap him! I'd murder the bastard!"

CHAPTER SIX

As soon as the helicopter—or *whirlybird,* as Joe called it—hit the ground, men began running from it towards Max and Rick. Six of them, Max counted. She'd expected one.

"Let's go!" one of them shouted.

"Hold on a minute," Rick said, surprising Max by the take-charge tone he assumed. "This isn't D.C. or Los Angeles. You can't just rush in here and think everybody is going to bow down at your command." He clucked his tongue against his teeth and said in exasperation, "Boy! No wonder David Koresh's mess turned out like it did!"

One of the men who had been in on the David Koresh deal in Texas had almost lost his job over the way the FBI had flubbed everything there several years ago. He cringed at the reference to it. All he had done was follow orders, and now the man who issued those orders was history in the FBI.

"Okay, fill us in. I presume you're the law in this hick town," one of the feds said. Turning to Max, he asked, "And who are you?"

"I'm as much in charge as he is," Max replied.

"A woman cop?" one of the men groaned. "I didn't figure we'd have to deal with that out in the boonies."

"Male chauvinist pig!" Rick spouted, surprising Max again. His devotion and respect for his mother was evident in his actions and reactions. *So,* she thought, *he isn't a wimp after all. Okay.* The realization somehow pleased her. She liked a take-charge man.

"She's as much—or more—in charge than I am," Rick went on to explain. "Her dad is the chief of police."

"Nepotist!" one of them grumbled, just loud enough for Rick and Max to hear.

"She's no such thing!" Rick said, jumping to her defense. "She works for the newspaper. So do I, for that matter!"

"The chief of police sent a newspaper reporter out here to get us? Doesn't he realize we are doing him a big favor, coming to some lost-world place like this, and we deserve at least a decent escort into town?"

"Sorry," Max said nonchalantly, looking at Rick to see his reaction. "He's a little busy. In case you hadn't heard, there's been a kidnapping in town."

"By the way," she said, motioning towards Rick's old rickety pickup, "you guys better hop in the back. Pop's anxious to get this thing wrapped up."

The men stared disgustedly at the mode of transportation. "You expect us to ride in *that thing*?" one of them asked.

"That or walk," Rick said, offering them the only option open to them.

Grudgingly, all six men—dressed in suits and the two with hats hanging onto them for dear life—climbed in. Rick boosted Max in, ran around to the other side, jumped in himself, spun the wheels and pulled out, nearly losing one of the passengers in the process.

"Want to have some fun?" Max asked Rick quietly.

He nodded, grinning broadly at her.

"Let's take the long way back to town," she suggested.

"You don't mean..." Rick asked, sure he knew what she was suggesting.

"Yeah. Let's go on the old road. You know, the one that follows the old river bed."

Rick veered the pickup around the corner, heading for the fun and excitement that lay ahead of them. He rolled his window down and hollered to the men in back, "Hang onto your hats, boys! It might be a little bumpy!"

****

In what seemed to the six big shots like an eternity, Rick finally pulled into town. They staggered as they managed to tumble out, one by one, of the pickup.

"You owe me a hat!" one of them yelled at Rick.

Rick went to the cab of the pickup and reached up on the shelf behind the seat, extracting a red cap with bright white letters forming the words "Farmer's Co-op" on it. He promptly plopped it on the agent's head, brushed his hands together and said, "Okay, now we're even."

Max turned away from them so they couldn't see her laugh. It looked like it might be fun working with Rick Brown. Yes, she was sure of it.

Bud Stryker ambled up behind the group, his hand extended cordially.

"Welcome to Willow Creek," he said.

"Are you the welcoming committee—or maybe the mayor?" one of the men asked bitterly.

"Actually, both, I guess," Bud said. It was true. Since he was about the only guy in town who was civic-minded enough to ever run for public office, he was always elected. "But I'm not here in either of those capacities today. I am Bud Stryker, Chief of Police. And you, I assume, are the team the FBI sent to help in our little kidnapping."

Max chuckled. He made it sound like it was the proudest possession the town had. Well, maybe that wasn't so far off base; it was certainly the most notable event she could remember in Willow Creek. Except the time the moose got loose and killed poor old Pete. That even made the news on Paul Harvey.

"Thanks for bringin' 'em in, kids," he called to Max and Rick, waving them off.

They could take a hint. They knew when they weren't wanted. It didn't matter. They had work to do. It had been so mucky when they tried to get out to see Paul Bunyan that they had given up in exasperation and defeat. Now it had started to rain, so if luck was with them, Paul Bunyan would be forced to come back into town early. If he did, they wanted to be *his* welcoming committee too.

"Let's take my car," Max suggested. "It's a whole lot easier to get into."

"I rather like the way you get into my truck," Rick said, winking at her, "but I'll give in this time."

Max turned to look at him. There was a twinkle in his eyes that danced like the first star on a cold, crisp, clear winter night.

"Just get in!" she ordered.

"Yes, ma'am. You're the boss."

Max was about to argue with him, but decided she might as well take advantage of the edge he was granting her.

Give her what she wants, Rick thought, *and make her think it's her idea. Pretty soon she'll be like putty in the sculptor's hands.*

"Where are you going?" Rick asked. "Sally and Paul Bunyan don't live in this direction."

"I want to swing past Beecher's Motel. I've got to change. There must be something in the water. I've gotten used to dressing like this, but now that I'm back in Hicksville, it just doesn't feel right. I won't be long."

She pulled up in front of the room she had taken at the motel when she had gotten a few minutes free earlier in the day. She jumped out and dashed through the rain.

"Need any help?" Rick asked.

"In your dreams!" she snapped back at him, disappearing inside. In a few minutes she emerged, like a butterfly. No, he decided, it was like a butterfly in reverse. She was clad in a pair of the tightest blue jeans Rick had ever seen on anybody and a sweatshirt so loose she seemed to be drowning in it.

As she climbed into the car, Rick let out a long, low wolf whistle.

"Oh, cut it out!" Max said, tempted to slap his face. "Keep your mind on business."

"I am," he said.

"Yeah, monkey business!" she retorted. "Now, where are Sally and Paul Bunyan holed up these days?"

"At what people call the old Larson place. They are renting it."

"What happened to Lars and Ruby?" she asked.

"They died," he answered. "Lars died in the morning, and in less than four hours Ruby followed him. Can you imagine anybody being that close to each other?"

"After that many years," Max said, "yeah, I guess I can. *Some* people."

"But not you?" Rick asked.

She didn't answer, but pulled into the driveway at the house. Paul Bunyan's logging rig was parked on the street in front of the house.

"Looks like we're in luck," Rick said.

Max just shook his head and mumbled, "I don't know what Sally ever saw in him."

"Don't believe in giving a guy a fighting chance to prove himself, eh?"

"Some guys could fight 'til their dying day," Max said, "and it wouldn't improve their chances."

"Paul Bunyan falls in that category?"

"I'd say so."

Wonder where I'd fall? Rick pondered. *Cut it out,* he scolded himself. *You don't need a woman in your life, and certainly not this one. She's not your type at all.* A nagging voice inside his head said, "Opposites attract."

Max walked brazenly up to the door and knocked on it. No one answered, so she knocked again, louder this time. She could hear noises inside, so she was sure somebody was home, and the odds were that it was Paul Bunyan, since his rig was there. She pounded again, this time calling out to him, "Paul Bunyan! Open up! It's just me, Max Stryker."

Slowly, cautiously, he opened the door just a crack to peek out. When he saw that it was Max, he asked, "What's that idiot doing with you?"

"Rick?" Max asked. "He's as harmless as a flea on a dog. He won't hurt you."

Rick cringed at the idea of anyone trying to hurt Paul Bunyan. The thing that worried him most was that if Max made any kind of accusations against Paul Bunyan, they might both end up as mincemeat. He didn't mind admitting that he was no match for Paul Bunyan.

"Okay," Paul Bunyan said in his big gruff voice, "come on in. But don't try any funny business."

Max and Rick went in. As she surveyed the inside of the small house, Max was truly surprised. Sally had never impressed her as being the domestic type. When they were in home-ec class in high school, Sally had been a complete flop. She was the only one who had a long, skinny apron after sewing the ties to the wrong ends. And cooking? Forget it! She even burned the milk toast! In spite of all that, the house was cozy. Even cute. Better than Max had done with her own apartment in St. Paul.

"Have a chair at the table," Paul Bunyan said. "I'll get some coffee."

Maybe it was her imagination, but he seemed almost pleased to have guests. She wondered if anybody else had been out to visit them since they had gotten married. She doubted it.

"So what brings you to call on me?" he asked, obviously curious. "I assume it isn't my good looks or charming personality that brought you here."

He threw his head back and laughed, such a deep, hearty laugh Max was sure she felt the timbers in the roof rattle.

"I'm afraid it's bad news," Max said.

"It's Sally!" Paul Bunyan shouted, jumping to his feet and heading for the door. "Something awful's happened to her! I just knew it! It's that damned Bill Crane, isn't it? I told him if he ever laid a hand on her again, I'd kill him! I swear I will!"

"Calm down," Rick said, trying to hold him back. "Sally's just fine. She's down at the bank working, just like always. Actually, it is Bill Crane who's in trouble."

"Somebody finally did him in?" Paul Bunyan asked. "It's what the poor sucker deserved. Who got to him?"

"We don't know yet," Max said. "Truth is, he isn't dead. At least not as far as we know. But somebody did kidnap him. Sally found a ransom note at the bank this morning when she got there. Whoever took Bill wants $50,000 for his safe return."

"He's not worth a penny!" Paul Bunyan said. "And it would suit this whole blasted town just fine if he never returned—dead or alive. Just ask anybody."

"You're probably right," Max admitted, "but Pops does have a case to solve, and he's called in the FBI."

"The FBI?" Paul Bunyan asked, rolling his eyes back in his head. "I don't believe it! Your *Pops* wants Bill Crane back that bad? Why?"

"He's got a job to do," Max said. "It's as simple as that." She hesitated, then added, "He was over and questioned Sally this morning."

"He thinks Sally did it? She's no bigger than a minute! She couldn't drag him off someplace and hole him up."

"Not by herself," Max said.

"He thinks I'm in on this? He thinks Sally and me..."

He stormed out of the house, leaving them still sipping on their coffee.

"Suppose we wore out our welcome?" Rick joked.

"Come on," Max said, taking Rick by the hand and pulling him out the door. "We'd better follow him, in case he causes any trouble."

"And if he does, we're supposed to stop him?" Rick asked. "Sure we are!"

By the time Max and Rick drove down the street, there was no sign of Paul Bunyan.

"He must have taken a short cut," Max said.

CHAPTER SEVEN

"That's weird," Rick said as he and Max approached the bank.

"What?" Max asked.

"That car. It's a stranger."

Max laughed. "You can spot a car from a block away and tell automatically that it doesn't belong here."

"That's not what I said," Rick said, shaking his head at the female line of logic. "He might belong here, but he's not *from* here."

"And how, pray tell, did you arrive at that brilliant deduction?" Max asked, her voice dripping with sarcasm.

"Elementary, my dear Watson!" Rick said, smiling. "I might not be the most outgoing person on the face of the earth, thereby avoiding making an acquaintance of some of the fine, upright citizens of Willow Creek, But when I first got to town I pumped gas for Hank. It gave me a first-rate chance to get to know what kind of car everybody in town was driving. Since Hank's is the only gas station in town, sooner or later everybody made it in there to fill up."

"Maybe somebody bought a new car," Max argued.

"Nope," Rick insisted. "If they had, I'd have heard about it from Gary. You remember Gary Johnson? Seems to me he has mentioned you. I think he had the hots for you when you were kids."

"I know Gary," Max said, ignoring the rest of Rick's accusations. "What does he have to do with anything?"

"He's a partner now in his dad's Ford garage. It's the only place in town that sells cars. So, if somebody had bought a new car, Gary would have said something about it."

"Ever dawn on you that somebody might actually venture outside the perimeter of our cozy little dive here to buy something besides a Ford?"

"My point exactly!" Rick said. "See the dealer's sticker?" By now Max had pulled into a parking lot right behind the topic of conversation. "It's from Edina. That's a suburb of Minneapolis. Nope, this guy's a stranger."

"All right, Mr. Detective," she said, "how can you tell it's a guy, and not a gal?"

"That's a cinch," Rick explained. "It's not a new car. It's a 1960 Caddy. That's a Classic, not just some old car. And you can tell from the hubcaps that the owner is somebody who really cares about it."

Max shook her head in despair, then pulled her car out of the parking space and made a U-turn in the middle of the street.

"Where you headed?" Rick asked.

"I think we better get Pops in on this one," she said, pulling the car into a diagonal space and jumping out. "Leave the motor running. I'll be right back."

Rick groaned. He had to admit, watching her sashay into the arena, that he definitely left his motor running! She was the most frustrating female he'd ever met. He didn't want to like her, but he had to admit that there was a fatal attraction he couldn't ignore. At least she showed some sense, going after her Pops. His mother, always undaunted, would have run in headlong on her own. *No telling who this guy at the bank is*, he thought.

In less than a minute, Max was back, her dad at her heels.

"Jump in back," she ordered her dad. He didn't take time to argue.

"You think he might do something crazy?" Bud asked Max as they drove the short distance to the bank.

"No telling what he's capable of," Max said nervously. "One thing sure, he's head over heels in love with Sally. If he thought anybody would hurt her, I wouldn't put it past him to try anything."

"Even murder?" Rick asked.

"Nobody's said anything about murder," Bud said. "So far, all we've got is a kidnapping."

"Sure wish you hadn't called those stupid FBI guys in," Max complained. "Now there's some other dope wandering around in the bank."

She turned the car off in front of the bank and ran towards it. Rick followed close behind. When she got to the door, she turned to look back and realized Bud was standing beside the car, not moving a muscle. She went back to him and asked, "Pops, what is it? What's wrong?"

"Listen," he said, putting his finger to his lips to hush her.

"I don't hear anything," Max said.

"I know. That's what scares me."

"You're not making any sense," Max said.

"I expected to find Paul Bunyan in there, throwing things all over the place. Maybe even shooting the place up, demanding some answers as to who did it to get Sally off the hook."

He glared at Max in disgust. "I don't know why you had to go and tell him, anyway. I told you to stay out of it!"

"Sorry, Pops," Max said, suddenly really meaning it. She thought she was so smart, and maybe she had messed the whole thing up. Maybe he had killed the whole bunch of them in the bank. She hoped there weren't any customers. At least that way there would be fewer victims.

"I'm going around the back to see if I can sneak in and find out what's up. *Don't go near the place! Don't even think about it! You either!*" he said, staring Rick square in the eyes.

"I'm not about to, sir," Rick said, his knees trembling at the mere thought of facing a room full of dead people.

Bud disappeared around the back just in time to avoid seeing the six FBI agents rush up to the front of the bank, guns drawn, and rush at the door.

"Hold it!" Rick shouted, surprising himself at the volume his voice suddenly assumed. "Bud says nobody is supposed to go in there."

"We're in control here," the head agent said firmly. "We saw some big, mean guy head that way and we figured there was trouble brewing."

"That's right, and he might be armed and dangerous," Max said, coming to Rick's aid.

"We're used to dealing with nuts like him," the agent said. "Come on, men."

"You'll have to shoot me first," Rick said, planting himself firmly in front of the door, blocking their entrance. "You won't kill a bunch of innocent people without even knowing what you're up against. Bud is probably in there already. Let him do his job."

"I wish Pops had never called them in on this," Max grumbled.

The smallest FBI agent snapped at her. "I heard that! Some female newspaper hound's got no business around here. Why don't you go back to the office?"

"And miss all the fun?" Max said sarcastically. "I wouldn't think of it." Under her breath she added, "Maybe if we get lucky, Paul Bunyan will shoot one of them."

"Maybe we ought to listen to them," the one they called "Dan" suggested. "They know how these people think more than we do."

"Whose side you on?" the head honcho growled at him.

"Life's," he replied simply.

Just then they heard a noise from inside. They listened carefully. It was Bud Stryker.

"It looks like it's safe now," he said. "You can all get up. Where's Sally?"

"Paul Bunyan came and got her," Mary said.

"Did he have a gun?" Bud asked.

"Don't ask me," Gerry said. "When I saw him standing there—so big and mad—I didn't think to ask him. If Paul Bunyan orders me to do something, I'm sure enough going to do what he says."

"Me too," Karyn said. There were tears running down her cheeks. Bud laughed, in spite of the seriousness of the situation.

"What's so funny?" Karyn asked.

"I've never seen you with your warpaint all smeared up," he said. "So you're not perfect after all."

She walked over to him and hit him a good hard punch on the shoulder.

"I've never been this scared before!" she said, wiping her face with a Kleenex she pulled out of a box on the counter. "And I hope I never am again! You'd better go out and catch your bad guy."

"Did he say he took Bill?" Bud asked.

"Well, no," Mary said, "but the way he was acting, he must have. Him and Sally. You know she's never been quite right since she married him."

"Sally?" Bud said, laughing. "I've known her since the day she was born. She's never been quite right, and it had nothing to do with marryin' Paul Bunyan." He turned to Mary, who was the head cashier. "Some stranger come in here lately?" he asked.

"Oh!" she said, running towards the vault. "I forgot about him!"

"Him who?" Bud asked.

"Tom Garborg. He's the guy from the bank commissioner's office that married Carol Dry. Remember? Seems as soon as the commissioner got wind of the kidnapping, he sent one of his goons up here to make sure things run okay. Well, I guess it's better it's him than some stranger. I'm sure Carol has filled him in on Bill Crane and all his *attributes*."

The huge steel door creaked and Tom Garborg stuck his head out, looking over the entire bank.

"Is he gone?" Tom asked.

"Who?" Bud countered.

"That giant!" Tom said, his face still white with fear.

"You mean Paul Bunyan?" Bud asked. "He's just a local lumberjack. He won't hurt you as long as you don't do him any harm. Him or Sally."

"Sally?" Tom asked.

"One of the tellers here. She's found the ransom note this morning."

"Boy, it's been a long day already," Rick said, moving away from the door when he thought the danger was past. The FBI men all charged ahead, their guns still drawn, shouting.

"What in the world do you think you're doing?" Bud asked.

"We're here now," the head agent said. "We'll take charge."

"Of what?" Bud asked.

"The situation," the agent replied.

"Situation?" Bud asked. "Yeah, situation comedy!"

"Yeah," Max said, poking Rick in the ribs with her elbow. "Sort of makes you think of something the Marx Brothers might do, doesn't it?"

"Them or the Three Stooges," Rick said, snickering behind his hand. "Wish we'd have gotten a movie of it."

Mary pointed to an upper corner of the bank. "I'm sure the video camera caught the whole thing," she said. "Boy, this will be great! We can show it at the Wild Rice Festival next month."

"You've got a video camera in here?" the FBI leader asked.

"Yeah, the Sears catalog sold them pretty cheap. Too bad they went out of the catalog business."

"Does that mean you shot pics of the whole kidnapping escapade?" the FBI man asked. "Why didn't you say so? Surely you've already watched it."

"We don't have it on at night," Mary said.

"Why not? Nobody's apt to hold up a bank in the daytime. They'd break in at night, when nobody's around."

"I can't believe this!" one of the agents said, wiping his forehead. "I've heard of Podunk Junction, but I thought it was about as real as Sleepy Hollow."

"Sleepy Hollow's not real?" Rick asked, his bottom lip curling into a pout. "Aw, come on. Next thing I know you'll be telling us Santa Claus and Peter Pan are made up, too."

"Come on, Pete," the head agent called to one of the agents, "see if you can retrieve the film. Maybe it will give us some sort of clues."

"Yeah, if Paul Bunyan and Sally are the ones who kidnapped Bill," Max said.

"Can't see that there's any doubt about it," the boss said. "Don't you know that an innocent person doesn't have any reason to flee? And they've obviously flown."

"Fled," Max said, correcting his grammar.

"Whatever," the boss said, waving his hand in the air.

Max walked away from the group, got into her car and started the engine.

"Where you goin'?" Rick called out to her.

"Home," she said, then headed towards the motel. It would have to do as home until she rented an apartment. She plopped down on the bed and stared around the room. It was so empty, so cold, so impersonal.

The phone rang, and she almost answered it. Then she hesitated, sure that the only one who knew she was there was Rick. Oh, and Pops. Maybe she'd better answer it.

"Hello?" she said into the mouthpiece on the old-fashioned phone, complete with a rotary dial.

She complained mentally about the fact that Willow Creek would never modernize itself, even though they had survived into the twenty-first century. This phone was just one example of their philosophy on life in general: it's always been that way; it's always worked that way, so why change it?

"Maxine," her mother yelled into the phone.

Max hurried to say, "Good morning, Mom," then hold the receiver away from her ear before it got blasted.

"What on earth are you doing down there at that motel? This is absolutely crazy. You get home, right now!"

Max felt like a little girl getting a scolding for staying out too late at night. Or the time she had gone from one friend's house to another to another to another and her mother had tried to find her. "But I told every one of them where I was going next!" she had protested. She still remembered the grounding she got for a whole week. Now she was being grounded again. "Come home!" her mother had ordered. Well, she was a big girl now, and she didn't have to listen to her mother.

"I can't, Mom," Max insisted. "I'm going to get my own place. I need my space. I can't be trying to stay out of your way all the time."

"I won't bother you about anything," her mother said. "Promise."

Max knew that was a promise her mother couldn't possibly keep. It just wasn't her nature to keep out of the way of other people. Not Max, not Bud, not anybody. It would never work, and she knew it.

"I've got work to do," Max explained. "With this kidnapping there's bound to be a lot of long, late hours to put in at the *Herald*. I don't want to be a nuisance to you and Pops."

"Nonsense!" her mother protested. "Besides, your father will be putting in long hours, too. Maybe you can help him."

****

Max sensed a note of worry in her mother's voice. She had almost forgotten that Pops had suffered a heart attack a couple of years ago, and maybe there was an underlying reason for her to have come home at this precise time. Was it possible that for once in her life she had a chance to prove that she wasn't really a selfish person?

"Mom," Max asked hesitantly, "is Pops all right? I mean *really* all right?"

"Sure, he's fine," Maggie said, not sounding convincing at all, "but what difference would it make?"

"Mom! That's not fair!" Max whined.

"It didn't seem to bother you at all when you were off in St. Paul. You didn't even bother to come home when he was in the hospital."

"But I called," Max said, trying to justify her actions. "I was busy."

"Sure," her mother said, "you were busy. You will probably be too busy to come to our funerals!"

The receiver banged and for the second time in too few days, Max was left with a buzzing in her ear after her mother hung up on her. That was the second time she had done that.

She replaced the phone on the cradle and sat down. Not on the chair, but in the middle of the floor, her legs crossed in front of her. She hung her head and cried.

She wasn't sure how long she had been there when she heard a knock on the door. She jumped up and ran into the tiny bathroom.

"Hold on just a minute," she called out. She splashed her face with cold water to try to hide the tearstains, then went to the door and opened it.

"What do you want?" she asked Rick.

"Well, such a friendly greeting!" he teased.

"I'm sorry," she said. "Come on in."

He stood just inside the door, and she went to the bed to sit down.

"I'd offer you a chair, but as you can see, this isn't exactly the Ritz."

"That's okay," Rick said, sitting beside her—*too close for comfort,* Max thought. "This will do fine."

Max moved over slightly, trying not to appear too obvious at her discomfort.

"What do you want?" she asked.

"Well, I thought if we were going to help your dad on this case, we'd better plan our strategy."

Max's mouth gaped open. She must have imagined it. He had told her before that he wasn't a reporter. Now he wanted to play P.I.? What caused the change? Did she dare ask him? Or did she want to know? Not knowing which route to take, she sat in silence—a rarity for her.

"What's the matter?" Rick asked. "Cat got your tongue? What do you think we should do next? Come on, I can't do this alone. I need your help. I have a feeling that you're really good."

He paused, and Max noticed that he was running his fingers around the stitching lines on the quilted bedspread between them. He swallowed hard then added, "Like Mom."

"You admired her a lot, didn't you?" Max asked.

"Mom?" Rick asked, surprised at her straightforwardness. "Of course. Everybody admires their mother."

Max thought of her own mother. She had never done anything outstanding. She was just plain Maggie Stryker. Bud Stryker's wife. Occasionally, Max Stryker's mother. But basically, nobody. Just plain Maggie Stryker.

"Thanks," she said, not knowing what else to say. For one of the few times in her life there weren't any words that were adequate to say what she felt. She smiled warmly at him. "I'm glad I came home."

"You sure?" he asked, mischief dancing in his eyes.

"Positive," she said. She didn't say any more. She was afraid to speak. It seemed like such a new sensation. She was sure if she tried, she would cry. And Max Stryker was *not* an emotional person! Anybody in town could tell you that! No, Max Stryker was strong—in control, purposeful, some might even say overbearing and stubborn. Then why did Rick Brown, whom she had known for less than twenty-four hours, have this incredible power to melt her fortitude?

"I have to do something," she said suddenly, jumping up from the bed.

She began to take the few things that were scattered around the room and crammed them into her suitcase, which was open, but still not fully unpacked.

Rick watched with interest. He had never known anyone like her before. There probably wasn't anyone else like her. *Some things,* he thought, *when God finishes with one model He throws the mold away—afraid any more copies might somehow be inferior. Max Stryker is one of those one-of-a-kind things.*

"I've got to go home," she said, hoping that was all the explanation Rick would need of her actions, but knowing it was dreadfully incomplete.

"Home?" he asked.

"Yeah," Max said. "To Mom and Pops'."

She waited for Rick to question her. When he didn't, she said, trying to make it sound logical, "Pops has always taken his work home with him. If I am there, I have a better chance of seeing what he's got on the kidnapping."

Rick sensed there was more to it than that, but he would wait until she was ready to spill the details. For now, he would leave it alone.

"Fine," he said. "I'll go on back to the paper. Joe will be mad that we've been gone this long. Remember, we still have a job to do."

"See you in a bit," she said, waving to him as he walked out the door and back towards the *Herald* office. She didn't move until he rounded the corner and was out of sight. "Thank you, Rick Brown," she said softly.

****

Max didn't knock. She knew her mother would be home on a Friday afternoon. She was always home...she glanced at her watch...oh, sure. She'd be watching her soaps. She'd be home.

"Mom?" she said as she walked into the living room, after having deposited her suitcase in the kitchen. "Does your offer of having a wayward daughter who thought she could do anything—or everything—come home still hold?"

Her mother looked up at her, smiling slightly, one lone tear making its way down her cheek. "You bet it does."

I wonder what she's up to. The thought ran through her mind for one quick, fleeting moment. It didn't matter. She really needed her. Bud wasn't as good as he used to be, and that scared her half to death. Especially with all this new excitement in town.

Max embraced her mother. It had happened before, occasionally, but it had always been forced. Something that was expected of her. Maxine Stryker never wore her feelings on her sleeve. Was it possible that she had really grown up? That she had her priorities straight? That she finally knew what was really important?

"I have to get down to the paper," she said. "Joe and Rick are waiting for me."

She scurried into the bedroom—her old private haunt—with her suitcase, then rushed out the door.

"See you for supper," she said as she left. "Make it something good."

At last, Maggie thought as she watched Max drive away, *life will be like it is supposed to be. Even if Bill Crane is gone.* She grinned. *Maybe that's what it took to get Maxine back home. Maybe that's the way it's supposed to be, too.*

CHAPTER EIGHT

Willow Creek was buzzing with the news events of the day. First there was Bill Crane's kidnapping. Then word spread like wildfire that Paul Bunyan and Sally were missing. Was there a connection? Was Paul Bunyan behind the whole scheme? Did Sally know that when she called Bud about the ransom note? If she did, why didn't she wait until somebody else would be at the bank? It looked a little too convenient to be a set up. Or had they planned it that way to throw everyone off the trail? And what about Tom Garborg's sudden and perhaps too-obvious appearance? Was it just a coincidence that the only outsider—except the FBI men—was somehow related to Willow Creek? Or did he figure into the whole picture in some weird, bizarre way?

Bud sat in his office, surrounded by all six of the FBI agents, hashing and rehashing the clues they had.

Frank, the head t-man, lit up a cigarette.

"You work for the government?" Bud asked him.

"Of course. Even a hick cop like you ought to be able to figure that out. Why?"

"You ever hear of the Surgeon General?"

"Sure. Why?"

"You ask as many questions as a three-year old," Bud grumbled. "Ain't a whole lot smarter than one, either."

"Would you mind getting to the point?" Frank asked.

"Okay," Bud said. "Don't you know it's dangerous to your health to be puffin' on them weeds? Makes your breath stink awful, too."

Frank dropped the freshly-lit cigarette on the floor and ground it into the tile with the toe of his shiny black wing-tip oxford.

"Now pick it up and toss it outside," Bud ordered.

Frank obeyed, muttering as he went, "Man, what a grouch!"

When he came back in, Bud was busily writing in his little black pocket notebook.

"What's that for?" Frank asked.

"My report," Bud said simply. He did not elaborate, but he had been instructed by the FBI office in Washington to keep a log of any and all events, no matter how trivial and insignificant they seemed. Especially after such fiascos as the Koresh deal in Texas.

"Better make sure you get his name right," Marlow said. "It isn't Frank, you know. It's Francis."

"Yeah, like the talking mule!" Pete joked.

Bud crossed out the word "Frank" in his book and wrote in "Francis" instead. He looked up in time to catch the stern grimace on Frank's face. At least he knew how to needle one of these outside invaders.

"What do you make of the video?" Bud asked. He had his own opinions about that, as well as everything else that had happened, but he decided to keep them to himself, at least for now.

"Looks pretty open-and-shut to me," Frank said. "Your Paul Bunyan couldn't wait to get him and his girlfriend..."

"Wife," Bud interrupted.

"...*wife* out of town," Frank continued, as though he hadn't even noticed Bud.

"Seems too easy to me," Marlow said. Then he stopped, letting his implication sink in for awhile.

Bud studied him intently. He was small, with black shiny hair and deep-set eyes that could bore a hole right through you. He looked like he could have been a member of the Italian Mafia from New York City. No, he was too young. Maybe his father was, and this was his way of repaying society for all the ills the family had piled on innocent victims for generations.

"What do you mean?" Pete finally asked.

"I didn't hear Paul Bunyan say anything that might indicate that he took Bill Crane," Marlow explained. "I'll agree, he seemed relieved that the guy was gone."

"Downright *glad*!" Al suggested.

"Seems to me that pretty well sums up the way everybody in Willow Creek feels about Bill Crane," Dan said. "Doesn't seem to be any love lost on anybody's part."

Bud watched these men throw their ideas, observations and suggestions back and forth at each other for some time. Only one guy, Al, sat there and kept his mouth shut most of the time. Bud was almost convinced he was a deaf mute. Maybe he should have sent somebody after old Mrs. Evans to see if he could speak sign language. So far, he'd had one minor comment in over an hour.

"Well, Bud," Frank finally asked, "how do you read it?"

Bud shrugged his shoulders. "If you want my opinion, we'd probably be a lot farther ahead in solving this case if we'd gone over to Fran's and sat there for a couple of hours."

"Who's Fran?" Frank asked.

"*What's* Fran's?" Don asked at the same time.

"The beauty shop," Bud answered. "The only one in town. I swear, if there'd been an Indian uprising today, the whole shmeer could have been settled in less than an hour by the women over there. They'd have had the chief smoking the peace pipe before the first scalp was claimed."

"Sounds ominous," Marlow said.

"Call it what you want," Bud said. "You guys are welcome to use my office as long as you want."

He wanted to sound like he trusted them, but he wasn't stupid. Just to make sure, he went to the lone file cabinet in the office and tugged on the top drawer. Satisfied that it was locked, he headed for the door.

"Where you off to?" Frank asked, sure he was going to try to conduct this investigation his own way—without them. He'd worked with these small-town bozos before. They always thought they could do a better job of it than the big brass.

"Home," Bud said. "I figure I'll pump Maggie about the gossip from Fran's. She always goes on Friday morning. She probably knows something."

Bud walked out and got into the squad car—the only one in town—leaving the six men sitting in his office.

"Should we follow him?" Pete asked.

"What?" Frank asked gruffly. "And squat outside his bedroom window to see if he and his wife exchange pillow talk about the biggest case this town has ever seen? Probably ever will see."

Dan stuck the video back in the slot and turned the VCR on one more time. They all leaned back in their chairs and watched, just in case they had missed something the ten times they had already looked at it. Al yawned, nodded his head, and in less than ten seconds was sound asleep.

****

Tom Garborg laid his head on his arms, slumping over Bill Crane's big oak conference desk. It was, he mused, as grandiose as the man thought he was. Self-inflicted accusations poured over his conscience. *You have deserted Carol when the baby is almost due.* He was as much an outsider here in Willow Creek as the "goon squad" from Washington. He didn't know anything about the way this bank ran. Thank God for Mary! At least she seemed competent. What did he hope to accomplish, anyway? He envisioned his two-year-old Michael and instinctively vowed to become more involved in his upbringing in the future. He wasn't being fair to Carol—in her condition—leaving her alone with him.

"At least I have one thing on my side," he said aloud, not realizing that Mary had walked in. "The whole town seems to be a suspect. At least I have a foolproof alibi for my whereabouts."

"Which is?" Mary asked.

Tom jumped at the sound of her voice.

"I didn't hear you come in," he said.

"That's pretty obvious," she said. "You were a million miles away. Now, about your alibi?"

"I was sitting in the commissioner's office when the call came in about Bill's disappearance. So, it is perfectly clear that I couldn't have done it."

"Why would you?" Mary asked. "Kidnap Bill, I mean?"

"I wouldn't," Tom said, trying to defend himself. "I hardly even know the guy. I guess the only time I met him was at our wedding."

"Well, guess that lets you off the hook," Mary said.

"What about you?" Tom asked her. "Did you want him gone?"

"Me?" Mary said, her face red with rage. "Are you accusing me? I didn't have anything to do with it!"

"Methinks thou doest protest too much," Tom said, spouting the only quote he could remember from his college Shakespeare class. "I didn't mean anything by it. I'm sure you didn't have any more cause to harm Bill Crane than anyone else in town."

"How do you know he's been hurt?" Mary asked, suddenly becoming awfully suspicious of this opportunist. She wondered what lay behind his sudden interest in keeping the bank afloat. She could have managed just fine until...well, until whatever.

"I don't," Tom answered. "I just meant, the way everybody seems to hate the old guy."

They both heaved noticeable sighs of relief when Karyn interrupted them. "You've got a call from St. Paul," she said, walking over to the phone, picking it up and handing it to Tom. "I suppose the big boss wants to know what's going on."

Tom held his hand over the mouthpiece. "Goodbye, girls!" he said, shooing them from the office.

"Shh!" Mary said to Karyn. They both put their ear against the door and stood, straining to hear what was said.

****

Maggie and Bud Stryker sat beside each other on the sofa, spellbound by the tales Max spun about her life as an investigative reporter in St. Paul. Bud frequently asked questions, extracting more details from her about each case.

Bud Stryker had never wanted to be anything but a policeman. But, he had promised Maggie years ago, before she agreed to marry him, that he would never do it anyplace but in Willow Creek, far away from real danger.

Maggie watched the expression on Bud's face. She realized, listening to the banter her husband and daughter exchanged, that he was envious. While Max had simply been a reporter who chased after the cops while they chased after the real criminals—dangerous ones, she realized and shivered—Bud knew he would have to live out his fantasies through Max, who had been much closer to the real action than he ever would be.

"It's almost ten o'clock," Bud said, grabbing the remote from beside Maggie and turning to the news on the Duluth channel. "Maybe we'll hit the big time with our own little story."

"I don't think a kidnapping is a *little* story!" Maggie chided. "Even if it is Bill Crane and everybody wished he'd been gone years ago."

"Bank president in the small community of Willow Creek has been kidnapped," the news anchor reported. "Details when we return."

"Look!" Maggie shouted. "That's you!"

Bud, to Max's surprise, turned a bright crimson. He wasn't used to being in the limelight.

"You didn't tell us they interviewed you," Max said. "When were they here?"

"Late this afternoon, when you and Rick were busy at the paper." He winked at her as he said, "I was glad you weren't around."

"Afraid I'd steal your thunder?" Max teased.

"No," Bud said. "Afraid you'd blow the case wide open. Too soon. You know how the media always is—blows everything way out of proportion."

"Do you know who did it?" Max asked. "What's your best hunch."

"Everybody at Fran's figures it's got to be Sally and Paul Bunyan. They're obviously the prime suspects, especially since they've disappeared, too, now." Maggie made it seem so simple.

So that's what the consensus of hens who gathered at Fran's had decided. Well, they may have been right in the past, but this time they had missed the boat. Try as he might, Bud couldn't believe it was Sally and Paul Bunyan. Call it the infamous police *gut instinct*, or whatever you wanted to call it, but he had to keep looking.

"Hush!" Maggie ordered, although no one was saying a word. "Listen to what they have to say."

"I already know what I said," Bud said, smirking.

"Do you have any suspects?" the newsman was asking Bud.

"Everybody's a suspect until we know more," Bud answered him. "If we could prove you were around here last night or early this morning, we'd have to add your name to the list."

The newsman laughed nervously.

73

"Any further word on the ransom note?" he asked.

"Nothing yet," Bud said. "We are just waiting for further instructions, hoping that will give us a clue as to where Bill Crane might be."

"I understand he wasn't exactly the town's most treasured citizen," the newsman said. Bud wondered if that was a question or a statement.

"He may have had his faults," Bud said, "but that doesn't give anyone a right to play fast and loose with his life. Every American citizen is guaranteed his own personal freedom. This morning Bill Crane lost his. That's a crime."

The newsman closed the interview with a couple of comments and Bud started to turn the TV off.

"Wait a minute!" Max cried out. "There's that Frank guy."

Bud fixed his eyes on the set. He should have known he'd stick his two cents in, too.

"The FBI is here to expedite matters," he was saying. "Bud Stryker is a good, conscientious police officer, but he obviously has no experience in such serious matters."

"Boy!" Maggie said, extremely peeved. "Guess they don't know Bud Stryker!"

Max and Bud both laughed. She might be just plain old Maggie Stryker to everybody in town, but she was at least a very devoted wife. No, nobody dared to say anything against Bud Stryker. Not even if this was far bigger than anything he had handled before. He was perfectly capable of dealing with whatever presented itself, and a kidnapping was no different from any other case he'd seen over the years.

A thought flashed across Bud's brain. He hadn't even talked to Hannah Crane, Bill's wife. If anybody knew anything that might give him a clue, it had to be Hannah. She was as blind as a bat when it came to Bill. *Blind devotion,* Bud thought. *Love is blind.* Okay, first thing in the morning he would drive over and question her. She had to know something that might help.

Bud's attention returned to the newscast just in time to hear Frank say, "It seems almost certain that Sally and this Paul Bunyan character are the guilty parties. Since they have skipped out of town, we are hoping that these pictures will help in locating them. If you see them, please do not try to apprehend them. Call us at this number with any information you might have. Remember, they may be armed and dangerous."

"Oh, for crying out loud!" Bud sputtered as they flashed the phone number for his office on the screen. "Now they've gone and goofed everything up. They don't have any idea what they're talking about."

"You really don't think Sally and Paul Bunyan took him?" Max asked.

"Nope," he answered. He shut the TV off, got up and headed for the bedroom. "Goodnight."

Maggie got up to join him. "Sleep tight," she said to Max as she left the living room. She turned back to look at her daughter. "I'm glad to have you back home," she added.

"Me, too," Max said. She couldn't explain it, but she knew she meant it.

As soon as she was sure they were settled in for the night, Max quietly went to Bud's study in the basement. She took his little black notebook out and began reading the entries he had made during the day. "Yeah, Pops, I think you're right," she said, closing the book and going to her own room.

****

Tom Garborg left the TV in his motel room on. He sat down on the bed, pounding the lumpy mattress with his fist to try to make it a little more even. He leaned over and picked up the phone, got an outside line and dialed his home number.

"Tom?" Carol asked before he had a chance to say a word. "Is that you?"

"Hi, honey," he said. "I miss you."

"I miss you, too. What's going on up there, anyway? Did they find Bill?" She paused, then asked, "Is he dead or alive?"

"No, they haven't found him. Nobody knows if he's still breathing. The bastard doesn't deserve to live. Not after what he's done to...everybody!"

"I know," Carol said, trying to calm him down, "but don't go doing something stupid." Tom could hear her crying. "I need you. Michael needs you. The baby needs you."

"Don't worry about me," Tom said. "All I'm going to do is run the bank until they know..."

The phone went dead. He tried to get another line out, but it was no use.

Tom went out to the office. "What's wrong with the phones?" he asked.

"Don't know," the night clerk, a teenage girl chewing bubble gum and reading a book answered. "It happens all the time."

"How long until it's fixed?" he asked.

"Tomorrow morning. If we're lucky, that is. People don't worry about this flea dive too much. You know how it is. Nobody stays here unless they have to."

Tom walked back to his room. *Tomorrow*, he decided, *I'll go over to Carol's folks and see if they'll let me stay there.*

He pushed the door open, then froze. His suitcase was dumped upside down on the floor, everything in it in a disheveled pile. Who would be looking for something he might have? As he pawed through his belongings, he didn't notice anything missing.

"Not a robbery," he said to himself. "This is crazy."

He set everything on the chest at the end of the bed, put on his pajamas and climbed into bed. He reached over to grab the remote for the TV, but discovered there wasn't any. He grumbled about having to get back up just as he heard Jay Leno say, "It seems that a banker who's really a dirty old man in a little town called Willow Creek, Minnesota has been kidnapped. The FBI has been called in, and they claim Paul Bunyan is the kidnapper. I wonder if he rode off on Babe, his trusty blue ox." The audience laughed. "I'm not making it up, folks. It was on the news tonight."

CHAPTER NINE

The morning came too early, Bud Stryker thought, but he had to get over to Hannah Crane's before anyone saw him. He hated sneaking around, but he didn't need those FBI guys poking around in business that didn't pertain to them.

He laughed as he pulled his heavy wool trousers on. He didn't have anybody but himself to blame for their presence in town. After all, he had called them. He knew it was the right thing to do, but maybe Max wasn't so dumb after all.

He smiled at the idea that his daughter was back in Willow Creek. He was proud of her. She had set out to prove something--to herself and everyone else in town--and she had succeeded. Just because the paper she worked at went belly up didn't mean she had failed.

Besides, he thought, *she does seem to have good instincts*. She hadn't said so in so many words, but he knew she didn't think Sally and Paul Bunyan were guilty any more than he did.

Acting on an impulse, he tiptoed out of the bedroom and knocked softly on Max's door.

"Come on in," she called, rubbing her eyes. It was not even daylight yet, but that didn't tell her anything; sunrise in the early winter in northern Minnesota didn't happen until almost nine o'clock.

Bud poked his head inside. "Did I wake you up?" he asked, seeing that she was still in bed.

"No," Max answered honestly. She had spent a pretty fitful night, cat napping more than actual honest-to-goodness sleeping. "I kept turning everything over and over in my head. None of it makes any sense."

"There must be more people in this town who would like to get even with Bill Crane than there are church members," Bud said. "Any one of them could have done it."

"But there aren't many people who are strong enough to drag him off," Max argued, playing devil's advocate.

"Ever hear of forcing somebody to do something against their will?" Bud asked.

"You mean like at gun point?" Max asked. Somehow she couldn't imagine anybody in this sleepy little town being that desperate. Still, it *was* Bill Crane they were talking about. There were a few times she had been tempted to take drastic measures herself.

"Sure, why not?" But asked. "There isn't a guy in town who doesn't own a hunting rifle."

"But wouldn't somebody have seen them?"

"When was the last time you remember somebody roaming the streets late at night? Shucks, I don't even bother with my one night-check any more. No need to. Not until now, that is. Guess I'd better get back in the habit of it."

"That night Bill came looking for you after the football game I'd just as soon have taken my own gun after him. Reckon every other father in town has felt the same way at one time or another."

"But nobody did it," Max said.

"Nope," Bud agreed. "Not until now."

"Do you have any new ideas?" Max asked.

"Got one. Don't know where it will take us, but I want to go talk to Hannah."

"You think Hannah had something to do with her own husband's kidnapping?" Max got a shocked expression on her face. "I don't think Sally and Paul Bunyan did it, but... Hannah?"

"Now did you hear me say I thought she did it?"

Max shook her head. She was trying to figure out exactly where he was headed with this whole line of reasoning.

"You coming?" he asked as he backed towards the door.

"Count me in," she said. "Give me ten minutes."

****

Soon they were cruising down the street on their next step into this investigation. Bud seemed nervous, Max noted. What did he expect to find at Hannah's, anyway?

As if he was reading her thoughts, he finally said, "Never thought I'd say this, but you're pretty good, Max."

Max's ears perked up. It wasn't often her dad paid her a compliment. In fact, she couldn't remember it ever happening before.

"At what?" she asked.

"At this spy business," he answered. "You learned well." A proud smile crossed his face.

"I had a good teacher," she said, returning his smile.

"Huh?" Bud asked innocently.

Max jabbed him playfully on his arm. "You, dummy!" she said.

Bud parked the car behind some bushes about a block before they got to Bill and Hannah Crane's house. "Don't want to make the neighbors talk," he teased. "You know how they gossip in a small town."

"Hey, Pops," Max said, pointing at the alien car in town. "That's Tom Garborg's car. What do you suppose he's doing in this part of town?"

"That's easy," Bud said. "You haven't forgotten that that is Dry's house. Seems pretty logical to me that he'd stay with his in-laws while he's here running the bank."

****

Hannah appeared at the door almost immediately after they rang the doorbell, just in time to hear Max remark, "I always used to think Bill Crane had to be rich; he was the only one in town that had a doorbell."

"Bill?" she asked as she jerked the door open.

"Sorry to disappoint you," Bud said. "Have you heard anything from him?"

"No," she said, ushering them in hurriedly, then slamming the door shut. "Have you?"

Max thought Hannah's eyes looked sad. If she was married to a jerk like Bill Crane, she would probably be glad he was gone. "Good riddance to bad rubbish," Mrs. Kindred used to say about such people. Well, Bill Crane certainly fit into that category. But, Hannah had been married to him for years. Maybe, in some sick way she did love him—in spite of the things he did.

A thought struck Max like a bolt out of the blue. Bud was right; people in a small town do talk. Was it possible that Hannah really didn't know all the things Bill had done over the years? Or, if she had been told, did she choose not to believe them? You know, she told herself, the old adage that if you close your eyes tight enough the whole thing will disappear.

Max listened carefully as Bud questioned Hannah. No, she hadn't heard a word from him. Yes, there had been a phone call early in the morning asking him to meet someone at the bank. She took the call herself, but she didn't recognize the voice. She guessed she was still half asleep. He left in a hurry after that. He hadn't even taken time to eat breakfast. Yes, that was the last time she saw him. No, he hadn't called her. Yes, she was seriously thinking about paying the ransom—just to get him back safely. Maybe that seemed dumb to some people, but they did have a history together. After all, they had been together almost thirty years. She told them she was going to talk to Art Moore today about the legal ramifications of getting at that much money.

When he was finished, Bud closed his little black book, stuck it neatly in his jacket pocket, shook Hannah's hand and said, "Be sure to call me if you hear anything from him. Or the kidnappers. Or if you remember anything you might think would be helpful."

"Goodbye, Hannah," Max said, feeling real pity for the woman. Not so much for what she was going through since Bill's disappearance, but mostly for all he had put her through while he was here with her. It wasn't fair.

Tom Garborg crouched down in his big old Caddy when he heard them come out of Bill Crane's house. Was it possible that Carol was right? Could Bill's own wife figure into this whole scheme some way? It sounded too much like a made-for-TV movie to be possible. Still, the local cop was here to question her. *Probably just routine*, he figured.

As Bud and Max walked back to the squad car, Bud asked, "How did she seem to you?"

Max hesitated, recalling the visit. Finally she answered. "Sad."

"Worried?" Bud asked.

She thought. "No, not really."

"Upset?"

"No, not really."

"Anxious?"

Again Max said, "No, not really."

"Anything strike you funny about that?" Bud asked.

Max tried to imagine how her own mother would behave if Bud had been kidnapped. Her eyes would be red and swollen from crying. She would be a nervous wreck. She would have been to the lawyer to find out about getting the money the kidnappers demanded in a matter of hours—maybe minutes—from the time she saw the ransom note. It wouldn't matter if the whole FBI told her not to pay the money; she would never have listened. She would do *anything* to get Bud back.

"Yeah," Max admitted. "It does seem strange. I can't imagine any woman taking what she has all these years, but it does seem like she loves him. She did ask if it was Bill when she opened the door."

"Bill wouldn't have his own key?" Bud asked. "Or try the door first, just to see if it was locked? He'd ring the doorbell?"

"I guess," Max said, realizing that she still had a lot to learn about this investigation stuff. All these things had slipped right by her. She made a mental memo to be more observant—to look past the obvious to the implied.

"We'd better head on back to the office," Bud said. "I suppose those blasted capitol goons will be there waiting."

"Wish you hadn't called them in on the case?" Max asked, knowing the answer.

"I did what I had to do," Bud answered, "but I wish I'd have waited a few days. We could have had the whole thing solved by then. I could have just sent them a report."

****

Rick pulled into the alley and parked behind the *Herald* office. He had gotten way behind on setting type for the weekly edition with the way he had run around with Max the day before. He figured if he got an early start he could recover what he should have done yesterday.

His dad had been up early, too. They had a big order at the sawmill and he wanted to be sure it was ready to deliver on time.

When they had eaten breakfast together—oatmeal and toast, the same as every morning—Rick's dad hadn't asked him much about the kidnapping, but he had heard the rumors that Max Stryker was back in town and that she and Rick had been snooping around. All he had said, Rick remembered as he unlocked the back door at the *Herald*, was "Be careful, boy." It was enough. It spoke volumes. Rick knew he had been thinking about his mother and the way she had died. It was a dangerous business, even in

Willow Creek. He always told her to "Be careful" when she left in the morning, too.

Determined to leave the whole investigative end of the story to Max, he began pulling articles out and feeding them into the computer. Yes, he'd had his fill of cop stuff. It just wasn't his bag.

He sat, his eyes moving across the pages of the copy—some he had written himself and some that had been submitted by various correspondents across the county. His fingers moved mechanically on the computer keyboard, entering data, moving it from place to place, adjusting column sizes and adding headlines. His mind, no matter how hard he tried to prevent it, wandered. To Bill Crane: missing. To Max Stryker: returned. To Bud Stryker: dedicated. To Joe McGrath: retired—no, just tired. To his dad: contented. To his mother: dead. To Bill Crane: missing. To Max Stryker: returned. He went over and over the same people, coming to the same conclusion each time.

He shook his head and checked the computer to make sure all of the work he had done today was safely stored away. Then he printed something out, tore the sheet off, set it on Joe's desk, locked the back door and jumped into his pickup.

"Sorry, Dad," he said aloud as he revved the engine. "This one's for you, Mom."

He knew what he had to do. He headed straight for Bud Stryker's office. If he had read her right, that's where he'd find Max. Paper or no paper, she wasn't about to let this matter rest until it was solved. And she must have inherited some of her dad's instincts, because Rick knew she would stick to it like a fly to fly paper until it was solved. *Really* solved. Not just assuming Sally and Paul Bunyan did it. If he was ever accused of some crime, he sure hoped he'd get Max Stryker on the jury. She'd never give a guilty vote to an innocent victim. No, sir, not Max Stryker!

****

Joe got to the *Herald* office about nine o'clock. He fully expected to find Rick and Max both at work, especially after yesterday. They were so far behind. He had hoped for an extra edition this week, and now he wondered if they would make it with the regular issue.

He tried the door, and to his surprise it was still locked. He took his key ring out of his pocket, fiddling with the right one in the lock, sputtering as he did about still not having it fixed so it would work right, and pushed the door open. The place was as empty as the morgue. Nobody had died in months. "Slow on the news business," he complained audibly. He wondered, probably for the first time since Bill Crane had disappeared, if the guy was still alive. Part of him hoped he was okay, while the other part of him didn't give a hoot. If he was dead, well, as far as Joe could tell he probably got what he deserved. He was sure no Boy Scout.

He still kept a desk at the office, even though he certainly couldn't claim to keep regular hours any more. He saw the note Rick had left for him. He took his glasses out of his vest pocket, perched them on his nose and read, "Joe, Sorry I had to leave, but something came up. I'll be back as soon as I can. I did some of the galleys on the computer. You can find them in there and start working on the rest of the stuff. I left the copy from Cora and the rest on my desk right beside the monitor. Rick. P.S. In case you have trouble with the machine, there is a tutorial program in it. Just ask it the questions you want answered, and if you can't get any response punch the code for *Help*. You'll catch on quick."

Joe stared at the note and walked over to the computer.

"Of all the dumb things to do!" he yelled, as if the computer could hear him. "Leave the directions for how to run you locked up inside you. If I knew how to use you enough to figure out how to get at the instructions, I wouldn't need the damned instructions in the first place!"

****

The phone rang in Bud's office. Frank picked it up automatically.

"No, he isn't here," Frank told Joe. "No, Rick and Max aren't here either."

"Yes, I'll tell them to get over to the paper as soon as I see them."

"Wonder what that's all about?" he mused aloud to the other agents.

"I wonder where they all are," Pete said.

"And what they're up to," Marlow said.

"Talking about us, gentlemen?" Bud asked as he and Max walked through the door.

"You just had a phone call from the guy at the paper," Frank said.

"Rick?" Max asked, just in time for him to walk in and reply, "Nope, not me."

"The old guy," Frank said.

Bud walked over to his answering machine and punched the button to hear any messages.

"He didn't leave a message," Frank said, pushing the button to "Off." "I took the call."

Bud's face got bright red. "You don't have any right answering my phone!" he bellowed.

"Pops," Max said. "The light on the machine's still blinking. Looks like you had some other calls."

Bud pushed the button again.

"Chief Stryker?" a man's voice said. "This is Tom Garborg. Somebody broke into my motel room. Doesn't look like they took anything, but they sure made a mess out of my stuff. Call me as soon as you can."

"Explains why he was over at the Dry's," Max said. "Guess whoever it was must have spooked him."

Bud pushed the rewind button and played the message again. He let it run a little longer this time, and shook his head. "Nope. That's the number for the motel."

CHAPTER TEN

By the time all nine of them were crowded into Bud's tiny little office, Max felt like a sardine crunched into a can. *Aren't you glad you use Dial?* She snickered as she thought that this picture would make a perfect commercial for the famous soap. *Don't you wish everybody did?*

As she listened to the geniuses tossing ideas back and forth on how to track down Sally and Paul Bunyan, she realized that something truly did stink.

Bud's mind wandered to the federal agents present here. He knew he had locked the door when he left the office last night. Maybe he should accuse them of breaking and entering. Just because they thought they were important, that didn't give them the right to break the law. He was, as far as he was concerned, *the* law in Willow Creek.

He almost asked them how they had gotten in, then decided to just wait and see if it happened again. Maybe, with all the excitement going on, he had failed to lock it. It would be the first time, but then it wasn't totally impossible. He made a mental note to be more careful. He wasn't worried about any of the citizens, but he didn't know these outsiders. He should trust them, but he didn't.

"What'd she say?" Frank was asking when Bud came back to earth.

"Huh?" Bud asked. "What'd who say?"

"Bill Crane's wife," Frank said. "Your daughter says that's where you were."

Bud shot stabbing darts at Max. She read the reaction, but was puzzled by it. Was he planning to keep everything he learned a secret? She would know better next time; she wouldn't say anything until she had cleared it with him first. She hadn't meant any harm.

The phone rang, giving Bud an excuse to ignore the question. Hannah Crane hadn't said anything that would shed any light on the matter anyway, but these guys would probably read all sorts of stuff into her remarks.

Frank reached for the phone, but Bud stuck his hand in under his.

"This is still my office!" he growled.

"Grrrr!" Frank said, withdrawing his hand hurriedly. "Do you bite, too?"

"Only if somebody tries to steal my bone!" Bud snapped. "Hello? Willow Creek Police Department, Chief Stryker here. Can I help you?"

Max grinned proudly at her father. He was a cop—a good one—and he was nobody's fool. Not even the FBI's.

"You don't say!" Bud said into the phone.

"Hmmmm!" after a long pause.

Max wondered who was on the other end of the conversation, but she knew Bud wouldn't tell, at least not in the presence of so many strangers.

"It doesn't match anybody's?" Bud asked. "You're sure?"

"Okay, thanks a lot."

He hung the phone up and stood up. He turned to Max and Rick as he asked, "Don't you kids have some work to do at the *Herald*?"

"Yeah," Rick said. "I guess you're right. Joe will probably be going nuts by now. I left the instructions for the computer on his desk."

Bud laughed, a deep, throaty belly laugh. "Old Joe running that newfangled machine? I don't believe it! That's worth a couple of minutes, just to see it. I'll meet you both there."

"Sure, Pops," Max said, realizing he was much more willing to share his findings from the phone call with them than he was with Frank and his gang. She snickered as she thought about Jesse James and his gang. Seemed to her like Jesse James' brother was Frank. She wondered if they were as incompetent as this "Frank and his gang."

"If you're going to sit around here all day," he said to Frank, "make sure you lock the door when you leave. Never know what kind of scoundrels you might find inside if you don't."

Frank got the feeling Bud meant him. Well, they had jimmied the lock with the credit card, but they were within their rights. If they were going to find out what was in Bud Stryker's files, they had to do it when he wasn't around. Besides, they were much higher officials than the chief of police from some hick town like Willow Creek.

****

Joe was sitting at Rick's desk, facing a blank—but lighted—screen on the computer when Rick and Max walked in.

"I got it turned on," Joe said excitedly. "See? Now if I can just figure out what to do next."

Rick laughed. "It took you almost an hour to figure that out?"

Joe looked at the big old school clock on the wall.

"No, not really," he said. "I've only been here a little over half an hour. Good thing I came; you were supposed to be putting out a newspaper."

"Me and who else?" Rick asked.

"You and Miss Private Eye here," Joe said, winking at Max. "I might have known she'd hornswoggle you into helping her in her quest for the truth."

"Fact of the matter is," Rick admitted, "she didn't ask me to do anything. I decided it was something I had to do." He hesitated, then added, "For Mom."

Joe's eyes filled with compassion. He knew Rick hadn't shared the story of his mother's death and her life fighting crime with many people since they had arrived in Willow Creek. He was honored that Rick felt enough trust in him to bare his soul.

"I'm sorry," Joe said, reaching up to put his hand on Rick's much higher shoulder.

"It's okay," Rick said. "I didn't want to do it, but I've got this feeling..."

"What the cops call a *gut instinct?*" Max asked.

"Yeah. I guess that's what it is. I just don't think Sally *or* Paul Bunyan were the ones responsible for Bill Crane's disappearance. Not that they couldn't have done it, mind you, but I don't think they did."

"So who do you think is the guilty party?" Bud asked as he walked in just in time to hear Rick's remarks.

"I'm not sure," Rick said, shrugging his shoulders. "You have any ideas?"

"A couple," Bud said.

"Care to let us in on them?" Joe asked.

"What?" Bud asked, a shocked tone to his voice. "And let you blow the whole thing up before I catch them? No way, José! When I'm sure of it and have the culprit locked up, then you'll get your story, but not one second sooner."

"Fair enough," Joe said.

"I would like to know who that call was from back there at the office, though," Max said. "We could tell you didn't want to tell *them* about it, but you can level with us. Can't you?"

"It was Mrs. Kindred," Bud said, then maintained silence.

When he didn't appear to want to continue, Max began to pressure him. "What did she want? You can't mean that she had something to do with this kidnapping thing."

"No," Bud said, "but I did take the ransom note over to her to see if she could tell who might have written it."

Max laughed. "Let me get this straight, Pops. You took a typewritten note over to an English teacher to get her to identify the handwriting. I hate to tell you this, but you've really lost it!"

"How long has Mrs. Kindred lived in Willow Creek, Joe?" Bud asked.

"Almost as long as I can remember," Joe said. "In fact, we grew up together."

"And how long has she been teaching English over at the high school?"

"Just about as long," Joe answered. "In fact, I remember her working as a substitute teacher when we were still in high school, her and me, that is. She's just sort of always been there."

"Exactly," Bud said, then smiled reassuringly as he explained his line of reasoning. "I know the note was typed, but everybody writes with a style of their own. Max, you're supposed to be such a hotshot newspaper reporter; you certainly ought to know that. Just how many people do you think would know it was 'Dear Abby's' column if they forgot to identify her in a paper one day? Most everybody, I'd venture."

"Pretty smart!" Rick said, impressed by Bud's cunning intelligence. "So you figured Mrs. Kindred would be able to tell who wrote it by the way they phrased the words."

"You've got it," Bud said.

"Well," Max said, pulling her hands through the air like she was participating in a tug-of-war on a heavy rope, "would you care to enlighten us? Or do we get to stay here in the dark?"

"She went through the voting registration," Bud said. "That was easy, since she's the town clerk. Do you know that there are only fourteen people who still live in Willow Creek who she hasn't taught English to?"

"*To whom she hasn't taught English!*" Max corrected. "Remember who you're discussing."

"Whatever," Bud said, making a gesture with his hand that indicated it didn't matter to him about proper grammar. "Anyway, she said Joe was one of those, and Rick—you and your dad are on that list, too."

"And you and Mom?" Max asked.

"Well, since we know none of us did it, that narrows it down quite a bit. Bill and Hannah Crane are also on her list."

"Not much point in considering them," Rick said. "And what does that have to do with who wrote the note?"

"She swears it is nobody she has taught in her classes. Says they could never have disguised their styling that much. No, it had to be one of the fourteen people, she says."

"Who else is on the list?" Max asked. "I suppose Ben. He's retired, but he's too old to have been in her classes."

"He's been gone for over two weeks. He's visiting his sister out in Portland."

"Maine or Oregon?" Rick asked.

"What difference does it make?" Bud asked. "Either way, that's a half a continent away."

"Yeah, guess you're right," Rick conceded.

"And there's Rev. Wall over at the Methodist church. He's from Iowa, you know."

"Yeah," Joe said, "but following Mrs. Kindred's line of reasoning, he writes a little column in the *Herald* every week, and I can tell you right now he didn't write that note."

"How can you be so sure?" Bud asked.

"Because he can't spell worth sour apples," Joe said, "and when I got a glance at the note, there wasn't a misspelled word in it."

"Observant," Bud said. "Glad you're on our team."

"Didn't know I was," Joe said, but the pleased look on his face expressed his glee at being included on the "inside."

"What about Paul Bunyan?" Rick asked. "I heard he dropped out of school."

"That's right," Bud said, "but she says that was after his freshman year. She taught him freshman English. She says there's an outside chance he could have written it. She claims he was the most creative writer she ever had in her classes. A real vivid imagination." He laughed. "She even said maybe he's writing some of those hot steamy romances under some pseudonym."

They all laughed with him. The thought of Paul Bunyan, big, gruff and strong, writing such tender love stories was more than any of them could imagine.

"Maybe that's the side of him Sally saw," Max said, causing them all to stop and think.

"Maybe he is our man after all," Bud said.

They all looked at each other. Could it be? Was he the guilty party? It was Sally who found the note. They could be in cahoots.

"Naw!" they all said in unison, as if they could read each other's thoughts—all the same. They couldn't explain why, but Paul Bunyan definitely wasn't the guilty party. All they had to do was to prove who did it so he wouldn't get framed by those stupid FBI guys who thought they knew everything. They might know Washington, D.C. or New York City, but they didn't know *anything* about Willow Creek, Minnesota.

They quickly discussed the other five members of Mrs. Kindred's list, ruling each one out as they passed over them. Sister Agnes, the retired nun who inherited her father's cabin overlooking the lake: she was so busy painting her pictures she never left the premises. Old Doc Hammond: he couldn't drag himself out of bed anymore to deliver a baby if it came in "off hours"; since the kidnapping occurred early in the morning, he couldn't have done it. Alvira Meyers: she was in a wheelchair and she waited each morning for the county health nurse to come and get her into it. Then there were Petey and Buzz Saw Zelman: they had lived with their parents until the old folks died. They were weird, there was no doubt about that, but they were as harmless as a newborn kitten. They were wards of the state, but the social workers had agreed to let them live on the old homestead. They wouldn't know what to do with Bill Crane if he was standing on their front porch.

"Doesn't leave much for options, does it?" Bud asked, scratching his head. "I've got this funny feeling."

"What about Tom Garborg?" Max suggested. "We have to find out who was snooping in his stuff."

"Later," Bud said. "Can't be too important. He's sort of..."

"Paranoid?" Rick said, remembering his reaction at the bank after Paul Bunyan had been there.

"Yeah," Bud said as he walked out the door. "First I've got to check out that phone call Bill Crane got."

"You think you can find out where the call came from yesterday morning?" Rick asked.

"If I'm lucky," Bud replied. "So much for automation and modern technology. If Norma was still running the switchboard the old way, she'd know exactly who made that call."

Joe stared at Max and Rick to see if they would follow Bud. To his relief, they both went to their desks to start working on the biggest edition of the Willow Creek *Herald* they had ever put out.

CHAPTER ELEVEN

Bill Crane's shaggy gray hair fell over his eyes as his head drooped onto his chest, awakening him with a start. He blew upwards, hoping to keep it from tickling. He snorted as he made a silent wish that he had kept the crew cut he sported years ago when he was in the army.

Frustrated, he gave up, surrendering to the lot he was facing in his life. He had always been in control of everything and everyone he wanted to dominate, but now he was in control of nothing. Not even himself.

Every muscle in his body ached. He had struggled as hard and as long as he could to try to free himself from the handcuffs that held each hand to their respective side of the cold metal chair. At least she hadn't pinned them behind him; that would be even more miserable.

He pulled at the ropes around his ankles, firmly attached to the chair legs. Knowing almost immediately that he would not make any more headway than he had in his previous attempts, he soon aborted that effort as well.

His instincts told him that it was beginning to snow outside. He was not in a position where he could see the one wall in the room that had a window. He would have to do a complete 180 with his head to catch a glimpse of the outside world. He listened closely; he was sure he could hear snow. He had never thought about it before, but as he pondered it now he wondered if anyone else had ever actually *heard* the soft fluffy white flakes.

He knew every nook and cranny of this cabin. He had planned so many things here. His fantasies had all been lived out here, but only in his own mind. He had often thought of bringing some of the young women from Willow Creek out here, where he could persuade them to partake of other-worldly escapades of which he had dreamed.

If she was trying to get him to take stock of himself, she was certainly succeeding. He hated what he had become. If he died here, alone, and no one ever found him, it would somehow be just and fair. He deserved everything he was getting now, but he prayed for salvation. He knew it was probably too late to save his soul, but if he could at least save his body—and his mind.

He twisted his head, craning to see his watch. Nine-thirty three. If she was true to her pattern, she would be here in about three hours with some food. As she did the three separate times she had come yesterday, if he was lucky she would release him for a few minutes so he could go to the bathroom, all the time holding the gun on him to make sure he didn't try anything funny.

He was bigger than she was. If he timed it just right, he should be able to overtake her and get the gun away from her. He didn't want to hurt her. He couldn't bring himself to hate her, in spite of what she was doing to him. He had certainly done more than his share of hurting her already.

He passed over and over the scene of his last morning at home. He heard the phone ringing. It was so real in his own mind and thoughts he jumped, thinking the phone was truly ringing here, but then shaking his head as he realized there was no phone here.

That phone call! Did she have an accomplice? How had she managed it? He saw himself rushing to the bank, afraid something terrible had happened. Maybe somebody had broken in and robbed it. Compared to this, that would be a misdemeanor and this was a major felony. How had she gotten in? Only the bank officers had keys, and she sure had no business there.

It seemed like a thousand years had passed since he had been forced at gunpoint into the car and brought here. He didn't know she even knew about this place. How had she found it? Did she honestly believe he had brought all of his *conquests*—albeit imaginary—here? Away from civilization? Where no one would be the wiser?

By now everyone knew about his disappearance. She had even made him type out his own ransom note! And such a demand! Fifty thousand dollars! Nobody in town had that kind of money except him.

Would Hannah really manage to get at the money? *His* money? Or would she even want him back? It would serve him right if she just let him rot here. He had taken her for granted all those years. Was he worth it to her? Was he worth anything—to anybody? He couldn't blame her if she ignored the demand.

Who found the ransom note? Surely they had called Bud in on it as soon as they did. Or did all the women in Willow Creek hate him so much for what he had done, or tried to do to them that they figured it was just a good riddance?

Would Bud ever be able to figure out where this cabin was? Even if he did, why would he ever think to look in his own place for him? Nobody ever kidnapped somebody and then held them a prisoner in their own home. The mere idea was absurd. He wished Bud had come here on some of the hunting expeditions he had gone on with some of the other men in town. Then somebody might at least know the place existed.

****

The chair creaked as the old man tilted it back on its rear legs. The tarpaper on his shack tore a little more as his head rested against it. He reached down and patted Cock-A-Doodle-Doo, his pet rooster.

He grinned at the thought that it felt good to have clean longjohns on. He always changed them twice a year, and with winter coming on, it was that time of year. Spring was the other time. *Luxury*, he thought. *Pure, simple unadulterated luxury.*

He snapped the chair back down to all fours when he heard the car racing past on the road that was about a quarter of a mile from his home. It was the second day in a row that there had been action at the hunting cabin. He had been tempted to go yesterday to see what was going on, but he figured it was the banker from town there with some of his buddies. He didn't want anything to do with them. They drank far too much and were way too rowdy for his taste.

Something isn't right, he thought this time. He hadn't heard any noise last night, and there had been only one car. He had stood behind a tree and watched as it pulled away, and he made a mental notation that it wasn't the banker's jeep, which is what he always used when he came. No, it was a pretty snazzy car, and things just weren't adding up.

Alex Broquist reached around behind him and pulled the tiny dog collar and the leash off the hook on the doorframe of the shack. He snapped it around the rooster's neck and together they walked out closer to the road to see what was going on.

"Cock..." Cock-A-Doodle-Doo began to crow, but Alex quickly grabbed his beak to silence him.

"We don't want them to know we are here," he warned, as if the rooster understood every word he said. Maybe he did; after all they were used to conversing with one another on a regular basis.

As the car hurried towards the cabin, skidded to a stop and the door opened, he quietly made his way closer so he could see what was happening. He gave Cock-A-Doodle-Doo a "hush" sign with his finger to his lips as he observed a woman getting out of the car and going into the cabin.

Alex inched still closer, straining to hear the conversation inside. He had always kept to himself, but he was a firm believer that the man who talked the least heard the most. On the rare occasions when he would wander in to Willow Creek for supplies, he heard plenty. One of the things that was most often repeated within ear shot was about the latest capers of Bill Crane, the bank president.

He guessed that the woman inside was Mrs. Crane, and he wondered just how much she had suffered at Bill Crane's hands.

For the first time in many years, Alex's mind wandered back to the late 20s, when he was just a youngster. He had stood outside his parents' bedroom door, listening as his father beat his mother. Usually it was after he had had too much to drink, which explained Alex's hatred for booze.

He had not meant to desert his mother and leave her to face the danger alone, but he just couldn't take it anymore. He had run away from home and stowed away on a ship to America. He had not even thought about England for many years. It was not a happy memory when he did.

He shushed Cock-A-Doodle-Doo again, although it was Alex who was chuckling. He wanted to stand up and applaud her. He was only getting what he deserved. If he had any guts at all, he would go inside and help her.

He listened, his mind whirring with plots and ideas. No, he would wait until she was gone. Then he could go inside and...

****

At long last Bill heard the sound of tires crunching on the fresh, crisp snow. That meant it was getting colder outside. Maybe he could get out of here this time. He *had* to get out of here. He would fight with her until he had the gun. He would agree not to press charges and even keep the identity of his abductor a secret if she would just get him back to safety.

Was his size and strength his best weapon? Or was it his ability of persuasion and reasoning? He would try that first, and if it failed, then he would go for the physical plan. Either way, one or the other had to work. If he lost this battle and it kept getting colder he would lose the whole war.

He shivered—not from the cold as much as from sheer terror of his options.

CHAPTER TWELVE

The engine stopped, the car door slammed, and he could hear the small quick footsteps as she approached the cabin.

She opened the door, her arms laden with bags. The smell of food nearly made him gag. It made no sense at all, but he was so hungry he couldn't stand the sight of food.

"Hi!" she greeted him, all too cheerfully.

He coughed, then opened his mouth to speak. His throat was so dry, he was so near a state of dehydration, he could not force a sound out.

"Cat got your tongue?" she cackled in a witchy tone.

"Water!" he finally managed to squeak out.

She went to the hand pump and forced the handle up and down, up and down, until some rusty-colored water seeped out. She slowly took a glass out of the orange crate cupboards and let the water drip into it.

Glad I always turned them upside down, Bill thought. *At least they weren't full of dirt on the inside, too.*

"Here you are," she said, holding the smelly liquid up to his lips. "Drink." It was an order, not an invitation. He gladly obeyed; at least it was moisture. It burned as it crept over his tongue and down his throat.

"Would you like to go to the bathroom?" she asked—too kindly, her voice full of sarcasm. "Do you really have to go?"

He had tried to put it out of his mind, but now, with the addition of water to his body, his need was more than urgent. If she didn't let him free to go, he knew he couldn't be responsible for the consequences.

"Yes, please," he begged.

Slowly, deliberately, she reached into her purse and took out her keys—the keys that held his freedom. He knew instinctively which one it was. That tiny little brass key would unlock his hands.

In an act of utter disgust, she placed the key ring in his mouth, letting him control his own destiny, his own imprisonment, yet he was totally helpless to free himself. She then bent down and untied the ropes from around his feet.

He stretched them out, wondering if he could get into a position where he could kick her feet out from under her, thus giving him the upper hand. With his hands still bound, he quickly decided against it. He had to wait until he was free.

At last she freed his hands. He looked at her, then at the barrel of his own shotgun, which was staring back at him from extremely close range. He never should have left the guns here. If only he had kept them all at the house, safely locked up. But Hannah hated having guns in the house. She always had. Ironic, when he thought about it now. It was a gun—his own gun—that gave her the upper hand.

"Go ahead," she said, "but remember that I am right behind you. You've got no privacy now, Bill Crane. You can do your thing, then it's right back to the shackles for you."

He tried to stand up, but he hadn't realized how weak he was. Only one day, or was it two, and already he couldn't stand on his own two feet. He grabbed for the table to keep himself upright. Slowly, like testing the water in Willow Creek to see how cold it was, he made his way towards the bathroom.

"Okay," she instructed him when he was finished, "get back to your chair."

"But I need to move around," he began to protest. "I am so stiff and sore."

"Too stiff and sore for all the other women?" she asked.

So that was it! She was jealous! He never knew she cared that much. All the women were just a fling to him. Just a momentary challenge. He never meant to harm any of them. Especially not this one. He had to admit, when it came right down to it, she was his favorite. Always had been. Always would be.

"Too stiff and sore for anything," he admitted. He had always been powerful, but she held all the cards now. He was helpless against her.

"What about the money?" he asked. "Has it been paid?"

"And how would anybody have that kind of money lying around?" she asked. "Sorry, Bill. I'm afraid you're out here for the long haul."

"What about Bud?" he asked. "Surely he's out looking for me. Eventually he's bound to find me."

"I think he's looking in the wrong places," she said, grinning ruthlessly at him. "He's convinced Sally and Paul Bunyan are behind this whole plot. He's busy chasing them down."

"What do you mean, *chasing them down*?"

"It was pretty convenient, actually," she said, that devilish gleam still in the corner of her eyes. "As soon as he questioned them, they split. Got out of town. Made them look *real* guilty, especially considering that Sally found your note and called Bud. It made it look like it was a scheme they had cooked up, and she would look real innocent by calling the cops herself."

Bill waited for her to go on. He didn't know what to say. He knew he had tried to make time with Sally as recently as last week. If Paul Bunyan found out about it...well, he probably wouldn't have stopped at kidnapping; he would rather have killed him.

"What about the money?" he asked, remembering the ransom note she had forced him to write. "I'll sign a note okaying the withdrawal from my account. You can divide it with all of them. I'd gladly give up every cent I own to get back home."

She laughed. He never knew she could be so wicked.

"What, and take the fun out of it? No, I think it's far more exciting to wait to see how creative you can be. You know, you really are boring. A stuffed shirt. Yes, that's it. Let's see just what kind of brilliant scheme you can concoct now."

Maybe somebody would take pity on him and figure out a way to come up with the ransom money. It looked like he couldn't take matters into his own hands. He had never been at such a loss; he always controlled everything—his own fate, as well as that of others. Now he couldn't even see his own way clear of this mess. For the first time in his life, he was honestly sorry for his past behavior. Fat lot of good his penitent spirit did him here!

She reached towards him, grabbing at the handcuffs that were still dangling from around his wrists. He jumped back, trying to keep away from her, but he lost his balance and fell, hitting his head on the table as he crumpled to the floor.

She gasped. She didn't intend to kill him. She never even loaded the gun. Was he alive? Or had he killed himself? The first glance at the pool of blood under his head frightened her, then it made her sick. She raced to the door and got outside just in time to vomit. She had never seen so much blood. She never meant for it to end like this; she just wanted to teach him a lesson.

She went back into the cabin and struggled, trying to lift him back onto the chair, but he was far too big and heavy for her to manhandle. She had to get out of there before somebody found her. Not likely to happen, she realized.

****

If he should come to and be able to make his way out of the woods, he could just as easily claim that she had tried to murder him and there was nobody to prove she hadn't. She didn't want to spend the rest of her life behind bars. As a safeguard, she reached down and pulled his arms up, spread-eagle fashion, and fastened each one to opposite legs of the table.

A sudden *snap* outside the one lone window made her jump. Around the corner on the other side, the noise had the same effect on Alex Broquist.

Hannah went to the door and peered one way, then the other. She contemplated calling out to see if anyone was there, but quickly decided against it. If there was someone there, she had to get out of there. She looked around for a car, but none was in sight.

Satisfied that she was alone, she went back inside to take one final check on Bill. She pulled on the ropes around his ankles, kicking him defiantly. "That should hold you," she said as she left. "Pleasant dreams."

****

Out behind the cabin, Tom Garborg nearly ran headlong into Alex as he scurried to get out of Hannah's line of sight. He hadn't meant to step on that twig. He was relieved that Hannah hadn't seen him, but he didn't plan on some stranger being there, taking in the whole thing.

"What the..." Tom said, bewildered.

"Shh!" Alex warned, holding Cock-A-Doodle-Doo tightly in his arms. "Wait until she's gone," he whispered.

Hannah left the cabin, jumping into the car and racing the engine to a loud roar, then she shifted into reverse, swung it around and tore out of there like a wild bear was hot on her trail. She drove as fast as she could down the dirt road. The ruts she had made when she came before had frozen now, causing the car to swerve from side to side, making her grip the steering wheel as hard as she could with both hands. She couldn't afford to get stuck in the ditch now. Even if somebody did find her, what excuse did she have for being here? No, she had succeeded so far; she wasn't about to get caught at this stage of the game.

****

Once they were sure she was really gone, Tom asked Alex, "Who the hell are you? And what's going on?"

"Seems like she got fed up with him," Alex said matter-of-factly. "Can't say as how I blame her."

"You know him?" Tom asked.

"This is Willow Creek, Minnesota," Alex replied. "Everybody knows everybody. Except maybe you. You look like an outsider."

"I suppose you could say that," Tom said. "I married Carol Dry. We live in *the cities*," he said, referring to Minneapolis and St. Paul.

"Then what are you doing here?" Alex asked.

"I'm with the banking commission," Tom explained. "They sent me here to keep an eye on things at the bank until..."

"Until they get Old Man Crane back?" Alex asked.

"Yeah," Tom said. "But what about the old man? Did she kill him?"

"Don't rightly know," Alex said. "Think we should go in and check?"

"And what?" Tom asked. "Finish the job if she didn't?"

"What's your stake in all this?" Alex asked, curious as to why an outsider would have such hatred for a man he hardly knew.

And the story began to unravel as Tom Garborg told Alex Broquist—a total stranger—exactly what Bill Crane had done to his wife.

In return, Alex—who hardly ever spoke to anyone—poured out his heart for the first time in his life of the abuse he had seen as a child, his escape to America and how he had ended up in Willow Creek to keep out of sight of the authorities he feared would one day find him.

"You won't tell anyone I'm an alien?" he asked Tom.

"Mum's the word," Tom promised. "Now, let's figure out what to do with him."

They carefully twisted the doorknob. It was cold enough that both men were wearing gloves, so there would be no fingerprints left behind for the police once they finally figured out where Bill Crane was—if they ever did.

As they got inside, they tiptoed over to the body, careful not to step in the blood. They didn't want to leave any footprints behind. Tom reached over and placed two fingers on Bill's neck.

"He's still breathing," he said to Alex.

"Too bad," Alex said. "Shall we finish the job she started?"

"No point in us getting in any deeper than we already are," Tom said. "By the looks of it, he won't last much longer anyway. Let's just get the hell out of here. This place gives me the creeps."

"Just a minute," Alex said, reaching for the gun that was lying on the floor beside Bill. "Let's make sure it isn't loaded. Just in case he should come around."

He checked the chamber, finding it empty. He nodded, then they both left, knowing that anybody else Bill Crane might try to attack, should he regain consciousness and at least a modicum of strength, would be safe from his onslaught.

****

Hannah pulled into the little service station and went to the phone that was hanging on the post outside. She prayed that it still worked.

"St. Louis County Sheriff's office," the voice said.

She quickly placed a corner of her jacket over the mouthpiece to disguise her voice.

"There's been an accident," she said, then gave them directions to the hunting cabin.

"I don't know who he is," she said in answer to the deputy's question, "but I think he's hurt pretty bad. You better hurry."

She slammed the receiver on the hook, checking around to see if anyone had seen her. Satisfied that she was in the clear, she got back in the car and headed for Willow Creek.

CHAPTER THIRTEEN

Bud stopped over at the bank, hoping to question Tom Garborg about the break-in at the motel.

"Haven't seen him all morning," Mary said. "He's probably over at Carol's folks."

"I already called there," Bud said. "They haven't seen him either."

"Did you try the motel?" Mary asked.

"No," Bud said. "I guess I'll head on over there and check it out."

Bud went to the door on the unit that Tom told him he was in. The door was slightly ajar, so he pushed it open and entered. To his surprise, after listening to his description of the mess that he'd found, the room was as neat as a pin. The suitcase was on the stool at the end of the bed, the lid down. Bud went over to it and twisted the catch. It popped open, so he went to the other one, and it reacted the same way. He pulled out his big white handkerchief and carefully opened it. Everything inside seemed to be perfectly in tact. He lifted the corner of each item and examined them. Between each layer was a loving hand-written note that Carol had tucked in for him.

Satisfied that there was nothing suspicious in the contents, he closed it, grabbed the handle with his handkerchief and took it out to the squad car. After all, it was the suitcase that Tom said had been tampered with.

As he headed back to the office, something about the suitcase nagged at him. Finally it hit him; if whoever broke into Tom's motel room and dumped the contents of the suitcase out, why were all of Carol's notes back in between each layer of clothes? The natural reaction of someone who put things back in would have been to have read the notes, tucked them in together or stuck them someplace else—but all together, not between everything else.

For the first time since they had arrived, Bud hoped that Frank and his cohorts were at his office. Ordinarily, he would have to send any fingerprints he could lift from the suitcase off to Duluth for identification. Maybe, with these guys here, they would finally prove to be valuable for something.

"Glad you're here," he said, greeting Frank as he walked into the office with the suitcase in his hand. "Can you run a make on some prints for me?"

"What you got?" Frank asked, his feet up on Bud's desk.

Bud approached him and shoved his feet down. He glared at him, but didn't say anything. His feelings shouted loud enough to be heard, even in his silence on the matter.

"Tom Garborg called this morning and said somebody'd broken into his motel room and messed with his suitcase. I figure if we can get some prints from it, we might be able to tell who it was."

"Wow!" Frank said sarcastically. "We've hit the big time here in Willow Creek. A real live...sort-of robbery. I suppose the criminal took something valuable?"

"That's just it," Bud said. "He didn't take anything."

"I suppose we can run them in, if you've got a computer." He looked around the office, shaking his head at just how primitive Bud had kept everything.

"Joe's got one over at the *Herald*," he said. "It's hooked up to one of those fancy facts and everything."

"That's a *fax*," Frank said, "not a facts."

"That's what I said," Bud insisted. "A facts."

"What's the use," Frank said, shrugging his shoulders and reaching into his well-worn brief case and taking out a fingerprinting kit. "Let's see what we've got." In a few moments he had a thumb and forefinger print, as well as another complete set of prints.

"My guess is that this one belongs to Tom Garborg," Frank said. "But the other ones, well, let's see if we can figure it out."

They headed over to the *Herald* and easily got access to the computer. Rick was only too eager to help.

They sat and waited for several minutes and then got a return fax. "Looks like they're not on file," Frank said.

"What's that prove?" Bud asked. This was all new stuff to him. He'd never had to fingerprint anybody before. There weren't too many big cases in Willow Creek. Oh, except the time the moose... Well, you can't fingerprint a moose!

"Just means whoever had hold of that suitcase was never in the military, doesn't have a criminal record, and has never left the country."

"That leaves just about everybody in Willow Creek," Bud grumbled. "And I thought you'd finally be some help."

"Sorry," Frank said. "Now what?"

"Well, I've got to think on it awhile," Bud answered. "Guess I'll mosey on over to Dan's. I do some of my best thinking over a piece of Mabel's lemon meringue pie. You comin'?"

"Think I'll pass," Frank said. "I'm not sure I could stand the excitement."

"Suit yourself," Bud said and headed for the diner.

He was sitting on his regular stool, sipping on his steaming hot cup of coffee. Something—like an unidentified force—caused him to swirl around and look out the window just in time to see Hannah Crane get out of her car and disappear behind the door that led upstairs to Art Moore's law office.

He seemed oblivious to the others in the cafe who sat huddled in various clusters around the tables, each discussing his big case. There was no doubt about it; Bill Crane's kidnapping was the biggest thing to hit Willow Creek. It was the talk of the town. Even Pete and Joe were busily engaged in conversation, having set aside their usual game of checkers, which they always played on the red and white checkered tablecloth. In spite of the mystery that it evoked, the feeling was not one of sympathy. Everyone agreed that Bill Crane got exactly what he deserved.

"Do you think he's still alive?" Oscar, the local mechanic, asked.

"Don't know," Nels, the school custodian answered. "I heard there was a ransom note, but so far as I know, nobody's heard anything more about where to take the money or nothing."

"If the kidnappers contacted anybody," Oscar puzzled, "who do you s'pose it would be?"

"Hannah, I guess," Nels said. "She'd be the only one who could get that kind of money." He hesitated, then chuckled as he added, an evil grin on his face, "She's probably the only one who might want him back, too."

Bud's mind was replaying the information he had gotten from Dave Barnes about the phone call Hannah had claimed to receive the morning Bill had disappeared. It didn't make any sense. Unless...

Out of the corner of his subconscious mind he heard Oscar and Nels's conversation. Sure, that was it! She must have heard from the kidnapper. That was why she had finally gone to see Art Moore. She had to get the money in order to get Bill back.

He focused his stare more intently on the door to Art's office. He didn't want to miss her. It would be far easier to question her in the middle of the street than back at the office with all those FBI goons there. They'd think he was off his rocker if they knew what he was thinking.

The noise from the people talking in the cafe blurred together into one giant buzz. Images whirled around and around in his head. He felt like he was in the middle of a movie that was playing on a giant screen. He was part of it, yet he wasn't. He felt himself falling forward, but he couldn't get his hands up to stop himself. He saw the coffee slosh as he hit it in his feeble attempts to slow his fall, but he didn't feel the heat from it.

"Somebody call Doc Hammond!" Starlet, the waitress, yelled. "Quick!"

She ran around the counter, trying to catch Bud before he hit the floor, but she was too late. A heavy, deadening silence had enveloped the diner. The loud *thud* of Bud's body against the old wood slats on the floor was the only sound. Everyone stared in disbelief. He had seemed fine just a minute ago. Maybe less.

"He's on his way," Dan said as he replaced the phone in its cradle. "Said he'd be right over."

Starlet was on the floor beside Bud, talking to him, trying to get a response. She knew she wasn't getting through to him. He was as white and ashen as a ghost.

"Anybody around here know CPR?" she asked.

"Yeah," Oscar said.

"Who?" Starlet bellowed. "We need it, *now*!" She wished she hadn't dropped out of Nurses' Club when she was in high school. She heard they had learned all that kind of stuff.

"Just Bud, I guess," Oscar said. "He used it on Ben once out at the sawmill."

"Like that will help a lot!" Starlet said in disgust. She breathed a deep sigh of relief when Doc Hammond walked in.

****

The door at the *Herald* flung open and Nels came charging in.

"You'd better get on over to Doc Hammond's," he said, grabbing Max by the arm. "It's Bud. He's..."

"He's what?" Max asked, following Nels, figuring to get the explanation on the way. "What's happened to Pops?"

Rick was right on their heels, his jacket flying in the wind behind him as he struggled to pull it on.

All of a sudden the weather had turned nasty, like it needed Bud Stryker around in order to be presentable. With him down, there was no telling what kind of a storm might hit. The snow was blowing viciously, threatening anyone who dared to venture out in it.

"He was at the diner," Nels said, running down the street toward Doc's. "All of a sudden he just..."

"He what?" Max screamed. Her face took on an ashy tone as she asked, "Is Pops dead?"

"No," Nels said, relieving at least some of her fears. "At least I don't think so. He just sort of keeled over. Star tried to catch him, but she wasn't quick enough."

"How'd he get over to Doc Hammond's?" Max asked, puffing as she ran.

"Some of the fellows at the diner loaded him into Doc's station wagon. They went along to help get him out when they got there. They sent me over here to get you."

"Does Maggie know?" Rick asked.

"Can't rightly say," Nels answered. "I didn't wait around to find out. I s'pose somebody over at Doc's has called her by now."

The jogging exercise from the *Herald* office to Doc Hammond's house seemed like a ten-mile track, instead of the mere four blocks it actually was. When they finally got there, Max was in the door well ahead of the two men who had come with her.

"Doc!" she called out. "Doc! It's me, Max. Where's Pops?"

"In here," Doc Hammond called out, his voice beckoning her to join them.

Max stood in the doorway. She nearly collapsed when she saw the pale face of her vibrant father, lying on the sofa, so still he looked... No! She wouldn't think that! He wasn't.

He couldn't be. "He isn't dead!" she yelled, as if her words would defy fate.

"No," Doc Hammond said, smiling sympathetically at her. "His pulse is weak. He had another mighty close call, but he's breathing again. I've called the ambulance from Twin Valley. They should be here pretty quick."

"Has anybody called Maggie?" Rick asked, remembering that not too long ago his own mother had looked the same way. So fragile. So tired. So--nothing! Like an empty shell.

"I don't think so," Doc said. "I've been pretty busy."

"I didn't mean..." Rick said.

Doc waved his hand in the air. "I know you didn't, son. Don't pay me any attention. I get a bit crotchety when things don't go right."

"And this definitely isn't right!" Max snorted.

"You bet your life it's not," Doc agreed.

"I'll run over and get Maggie," Rick said. "Can I borrow your car, Doc? It'll be faster."

"Sure," Doc Hammond replied, reaching into his pocket and taking his keys out, throwing them to Rick.

Rick went over beside Max and put his arm around her tenderly. He understood what she was going through. God knows, he'd lived through it himself.

"You be okay while I'm gone?" he asked, giving her a little squeeze.

"Yeah," Max said. "I'll be fine. Just go get Mom. Hurry. She'll need us."

Rick felt a warmth at being included in this little family circle. He had only known Max a few days, but it seemed like they had been friends forever. He hadn't felt this close to anyone in a long time.

"Be back in a flash," he said as he disappeared.

When he was gone, Max pulled a straight-back wood chair over beside Bud and sat down, taking his hand in hers.

"Doc," she said, her voice trembling, "he's cold."

"His heart still isn't up to par," Doc explained, "but his pulse is getting stronger. That's a good sign."

"Is..." Max stopped, afraid to ask the question she wanted answered. "Is he going to..."

"Die?" Doc asked bluntly.

"No," Max said. "Is he going to make it?"

Doc smiled at her. "If you keep up a good positive attitude like that, he can't help but pull through."

"I'm here, Pops," she said, stroking his hand. "It's going to be all right. You'll see. Don't you worry about a thing."

Suddenly Max's mind went back to the kidnapping case. Maybe it was too much for Pops. Her mother had said he wasn't as strong as he used to be. If that was what had caused this whole thing, she had to put his mind at ease. Had to let him know...

"Doc?" Max asked softly. "Can he hear me?"

"I don't know," Doc said. "It's hard to say. A lot of times, even when a person is in a coma, they hear things that go on around them. Why?"

"Just wondered," she said. Then she leaned up close to Bud's ear, almost whispering. "Don't you worry about a thing, Pops. Rick and I, we won't let those big shot guys mess everything up. We'll get to the bottom of this whole thing. We'll figure out who's got Bill and where. We'll get him back, Pops. I promise. We'll do it for you."

Like thought transference between two lovers who don't need to speak, but who can read each other's minds, Max instinctively reached into Bud's jacket pocket and took out his little black book. Whatever answers he had found, or whatever questions were still unanswered, she knew they would all be contained in there.

A small moan emerged from Bud. Slowly, like it took every ounce of strength he possessed, he opened one eye and said, so quietly it was almost inaudible, "Hannah." Then his eyes were closed and he was miles away from them again.

****

Rick and Maggie pulled up in front of Doc's house just seconds before the ambulance from Twin Valley arrived, its red lights flashing like an alien's spaceship. They stood aside as the emergency technicians jumped out and raced inside.

"In here," Doc yelled.

By the time Rick and Maggie got in, all three of them were leaning over Bud, making him nearly invisible behind their cloak of white.

"Let me at him," Maggie said, pushing her way through. "He needs me."

The men elbowed her back, but Doc Hammond stepped into the picture.

"She's probably right," he said. "Family is pretty important to a patient at a time like this. Come on, Maggie. Let him know you're here."

Maggie bent over and kissed Bud on the cheek. "We made it last time," she said, "and we'll do it again now. You've got to stick around a while longer. You've got a kidnapping to solve. Remember?"

Max didn't say anything, but she was sure she saw a slight smile on Pops' face. Maggie was true to form; *nobody* could do Bud Stryker's job but Bud Stryker!

"Let's get him out of here," one of the ambulance crew said, pulling a stretcher behind him. "You did good, Doc," he said, nodding to the old physician. "He seems to have stabilized. It's safe to move him."

"Where will you take him?" Maggie asked.

"To Community Hospital in Twin Valley," the ambulance driver said. "He'll get good care there, and they can decide what he needs."

"We'll be right behind you," Max said. "I'll go get my car, Mom."

Maggie shivered. She had accused Max of not being there for her father when he had his last heart attack, but she knew what she had to do.

"Can you drive me to Twin Valley, Doc?" she asked.

"Sure, Maggie," Doc said, looking puzzled.

"Mom!" Max protested. "I can do it. I want to be with Pops." She looked somber. "This time," she said.

"No, baby," Maggie said, crossing the room to her daughter. She took her in her arms, something Max hadn't allowed her to do for years. "There's something else you have to do. For your father."

Max didn't say anything. She just waited for Maggie to continue.

"You have to find out who's got Bill Crane. It would mean more to your father than anything else you could do. If—*when* he comes to—he'll want to know what's happening on the case. I can't tell him those goons are running the show. He'll have another heart attack just thinking about it!"

Max nodded in agreement. She looked at Rick. "Tell him I've got a top-notch helper," she said.

"Will do," Maggie promised. There was pride in her look as she said, "You know what your father said last night?"

Max shrugged her shoulders.

"He said you are *real* good. He's proud of you, Maxine. Don't let him down."

"I won't," Max said, returning her mother's hug.

The ambulance backed up a few feet, then pulled out into the street, making a U-turn and heading east.

"Let's go, Doc," Maggie said.

Max and Rick stood outside and watched them follow the ambulance.

"You okay?" Rick asked, knowing from experience how vulnerable she was at this very moment.

"Yeah," she said, a tear trickling down her cheek. "I'll be just fine." She smiled through the tears. "Come on, we've got a kidnapper to catch. For Pops."

"You bet," Rick said, putting his arm around her protectively. Under his breath he said, "And for you, Mom."

****

The snow was whirling around in the air by the time Tom Garborg pulled into a parking spot in front of the bank. He went in and headed for Bill Crane's office, closing the door behind him. He picked up the phone and dialed his number at home.

"Carol, baby, are you okay?" he asked.

"I'm fine," she said. She could sense the urgency and worry in his voice. "Are you?"

"Yeah, baby. I'm great. Just great."

He hung the phone up. Yes, he was terrific. With any luck at all, Bill Crane would be dead within a few hours. He didn't stand a chance. He knew the gun wasn't loaded. He had no way to protect himself, even if he didn't die of natural causes.

CHAPTER FOURTEEN

Max got in her car, followed by Rick. He wasn't sure exactly where she was headed, but he didn't want to leave her alone. Not now. He'd done this scene at the hospital. If what it took to make sure she was okay was for him to stick his neck out all the way on this crazy kidnapping case, well, so be it.

"What's that?" Rick asked as Max reached into her back jeans pocket and took out the little black book.

"Pops' little black book," she replied, as if that explained everything.

"Let me guess," Rick teased, trying to lighten her mood, "it is full of the names of all the cute women in Willow Creek."

"No," Max said, laughing in spite of everything, "that's Bill Crane's little black book."

"All three of them are in it?" he asked, snickering. "Oh, I forgot. Now there are four of them since you came back to town."

"If that was meant to be a left-handed compliment, thank you," Max said, reaching over beside her and patting his knee. She skimmed over the latest entries in the book and let out a long, low whistle. "Get this," she said. "Seems like somebody broke into Tom Garborg's motel room last night. At least that's what he told Pops. Only thing is, when Pops went over there he couldn't find any sign of anything being tampered with. Everything in his room, including the stuff in his suitcase, was as neat as a pin."

"What'd he make of that?" Rick asked. He hated it when he was suckered in by her. He'd seen the same thing happen with his mom and dad countless times as he grew up. It always meant no good.

"Let's go on over to the bank," she suggested. "Maybe we can figure out what's going on if we can find Tom."

"Find him?" Rick asked, puzzled.

"Pops says he's been missing all day. He tried to find him just before he went to the diner and collapsed. That's almost the last thing he wrote. That and the fact that Maggie went up to see Art Moore."

"Why did she do that?" Rick asked.

"Pops figured she'd heard from the kidnapper. He was going to question her out in the street when he collapsed. He didn't even finish his last sentence."

"What if Tom isn't at the bank?" he asked. "What then?"

"Then I guess we'll have to call in the FBI."

"What?" Rick shrieked. He had to admit they weren't exactly his favorite crew. Except for the entertainment value, of course.

"Don't go getting your tail in a knot," Max said. "Pops got them to send off the fingerprints from Tom's suitcase. There was one set on it besides Tom's."

"Whose?" Rick asked.

"Don't know," Max replied. "Pops figured it was probably somebody from the bank. He was going to get fingerprints from all of them to see if they matched."

"What are we waiting for?" Rick asked, getting out of the car and taking off the block and a half to the bank. Max slammed the car door shut behind her. He could be so damned exasperating! She had a perfectly good set of wheels; why did he insist on walking everywhere? She smiled as she realized that before she went off to the big city she had walked every place, too. It wasn't like it was that far.

They entered the bank together. Max had figured out right from the start that Mary was pretty much in charge of everything since Bill was gone. Oh, sure, Tom Garborg was there to look like somebody was in control, but she had watched him call Mary in on almost everything he needed. He didn't, Max decided, know enough to run a race, much less a bank.

"Have you seen Tom Garborg?" Max asked Mary.

"No," she answered. "What's with him, anyway? He was so blamed anxious to get up here to stick his nose in where it didn't belong, and now everybody seems to want him, and for what? Sure is a crazy mess Bill got us into. Can't get any work done at all anymore."

"I need all of you to cooperate," Max explained. "We have to get the fingerprints from all of the bank employees."

Mary shifted her weight—all three hundred plus pounds of it—from one foot to another. Max made a mental note of her anxiety and nervousness. It was probably a natural reaction, but still...

"I'll get them for you," Mary said. Soon, five of the six workers were standing in front of Max, their hands outstretched like they were waiting for an execution.

"Who's first?" Max asked.

"I might as well get it over with," Karyn said, going to the front of the line. Rick grabbed her hand, rolled her fingers—one by one—back and forth over the black inkpad and pushed them hard against the paper. He then carefully wrote her name by the prints. Karyn scrambled back to the bathroom to wash the ink residue off. She sure didn't want to get any of it on her new skirt, which she had just gotten from the Neiman Marcus catalog. It was a designer garment, and she wasn't going to let anybody ruin it. Especially not Bill Crane! She grimaced as she thought that he had a way of ruining everything, even when he wasn't there.

The others followed suit.

"Is that everybody?" Max asked Mary.

"Everybody except Eric," she said.

"Where's he?" Max asked, knowing that with Bill gone he would be the only officer left in the bank. Eric Hanson was the vice-president, and a good, honest hard worker. Max almost opted for skipping him, but decided she would get his prints too, so that left only Mary.

"We can do him in a minute. Your turn," she said to Mary. Mary immediately began shifting her weight nervously from one foot to the other again.

"Surely you don't think I had anything to do with... Well, I didn't. I'm probably the only person in Willow Creek who doesn't have any reason to hate Bill Crane. Oh, I know what his reputation is. But I swear, he never tried to come on to me. Not once."

Max looked at her in utter shock. Was this the motive for Bill Crane's disappearance? Did Mary kidnap him, just because he *didn't* try to proposition her? Jealousy is such a nasty thing! Who would have thought it? She glanced at Rick, who seemed oblivious to the obvious.

"I'll go get Eric," Mary said, trying to put suspicion on somebody else. "He's in the back office with Hannah."

She went off in a huff, her face as red as a beet and her hips swaggering from side to side as she tried to run.

She glanced into Bill Crane's office on her way past it, spotting Tom Garborg at the desk. *Wonder when he got back,* she mused.

****

"You have to do it," Hannah Crane insisted as she sat facing Eric. "I talked to Art and he said it's perfectly legal. Go ahead and call them."

"I don't know," Eric said hesitatingly. He had never been quick on making decisions; that's why he was still a vice-president. Who ever heard of a vice- president who was important? "Just think about it," Bill had said once to

Hannah. "How many vice-presidents can you name? Most people don't even know George Washington and Abraham Lincoln's vice-presidents. And everybody would like to forget Spiro Agnew!"

"I have a power-of-attorney paper right here," Hannah said, waving her hand in the air. "I can sign for the release of the money."

She sounds desperate, Eric thought. Frankly, he hadn't missed the guy that much in the last few days. Bill Crane was more of a necessary nuisance, as far as he was concerned, than an asset to the bank. He never would have lasted as long as he did if it weren't for the fact that he had more money in Willow Creek than anybody else.

"I'll have to call a meeting of the board," Eric said.

"So call it," Hannah ordered.

Surprised by her take-charge attitude, so unlike her, Eric obediently took the phone and began dialing.

"They're all coming right over," he said after he talked to all the members. "I don't know if they will go along with this or not."

****

"Excuse me," Mary said, gently pushing the door open when she was satisfied that she had heard as much as she was going to. "Max Stryker is out front. She has fingerprinted everybody but you, and she won't leave until she gets yours too."

"What on earth for?" he asked, aggravated by the insinuation her actions contained. "Are we all suspects?"

"So it seems," Mary said, following him out to the bank lobby.

Eric willingly stuck his fingers on the pad and then on the paper. "This sure as hell doesn't make any sense," he complained as he went back to the office.

"Your turn," Max said again, turning to Mary.

"What do you want this for?" Mary asked. "You think one of us killed Bill?"

Max jumped back. "Who said anything about Bill being dead?"

She watched as Mary's face twisted in agony. She hadn't meant to say that. She didn't know if he was dead or alive. Before she meant to, she blurted out, "All I did was go through some of his stuff to see if he had anything hidden. I didn't do anything to Bill. He wasn't worth it!"

Max's mouth dropped open. "*You* broke into Tom's motel room?" she asked, putting two and two together.

"Whoops!" Mary muttered, wishing she could run away, but knowing that would make her look as guilty as Sally and Paul Bunyan.

"What made you think Tom had anything to do with Bill's disappearance? He wasn't even in town until after he was gone."

"So he says," Mary said. "Anyway, he's probably telling the truth. I found a receipt for the gas he charged in Minneapolis the day he came up here. So, it was a dead end."

"Will you please leave the investigating business to the pros?" Max asked. She shook with anger at this invasion into Pops' case.

"Like you?" Mary said, her voice dripping with antagonism. "You don't belong in the middle of it, either."

"Oh, go on," Max said. She turned to Rick. "Guess we don't need the prints after all. We know what we came to find out. The prints on Tom's suitcase obviously belong to Mary."

Tom came out from his office just in time to hear Max's last remark. "Mary?" he asked, surprise registering in his tone of voice. "But why?"

"You were the only outsider," she replied, as if that explained everything.

"So from the way I see it, that means I'm the only one *without* a motive for doing the old man in," Tom argued. "Anyway, thanks for putting everything back so neatly."

"If everything was back where it belonged," Max said, turning to face Tom, "how did you know somebody had been there?"

"Elementary, my dear Watson," Tom said. "I could see a spot on the bed where somebody had been sitting. Those mattresses are as soft as a featherbed. The imprint of *somebody's* butt was there, as plain as day."

"Just like Goldilocks," Mary said, flipping her hair from side to side with each shake of her head, leaving them all laughing. "And you honestly didn't know who had the biggest butt print in town?"

Max stormed out of the bank, frustrated to the teeth that everybody seemed to want a piece of the action on this case. *They really should leave it to the pros*, she thought, then chuckled, realizing that she was no more a pro than the rest of them. Well, except for listening to her dad all of her life, and her work covering the crime beat in St. Paul. That clearly gave her an edge. Lost in her own thoughts, she nearly ran into Malcolm Schwartz, the chairman of the board, as he came in.

****

When all five members of the board of directors of Willow Creek State Bank had arrived, Eric Hanson and Hannah Crane were seated around the big oak conference table where all major decisions had been made for years.

"So what's your plan?" Malcolm asked, looking headlong at Hannah.

"The ransom note," Hannah began, "said Bill would be freed for $50,000."

"And does Bill have that much in his savings account?" Malcolm asked, certain the answer would be negative.

"Well, no," Hannah admitted. "Not in cash, anyway."

She handed Bill's passbook to Malcolm. It showed a hefty balance—nearly $35,000—but that still left a difference of $15,000.

"And where do you intend to get the rest of the money?" Jim Patterson asked.

"If the bank will loan me the money against the securities Bill has, I'm sure he will gladly cash them in to pay it off immediately," Hannah answered.

Like an intruder, Tom Garborg ran in. He was out of breath and Joe noticed that his shoes were muddy. He sat down, uninvited, listening carefully to the conversation.

Joe had left the paper to run over to the bank. He was the secretary of the board, and they couldn't make any decision this important unless everybody was present. All were here and accounted for, except Bill Crane, of course. Joe muttered something about wishing he was back at the paper reporting on this stuff instead of making useless decisions. The longer it was, the more convinced he was that the old guy was already dead. His investigative mind, however, kicked into action.

"Where are you supposed to take the money?" he asked.

"I know it sounds crazy," Hannah said, fiddling nervously with the papers she held in her hands, "but the note says the money—$50,000 in unmarked bills—is supposed to be put in the dumpster out behind the bank."

She hesitated for several moments. Finally, struggling to remain composed, she said, "All the women..."

She stopped. She was so ashamed. How could she have let him get by with the life he had lived for years? She had known for a long time that he tried to prey on every young woman who'd ever been in Willow Creek. As far as that goes, it hadn't been just the *young* women. She wouldn't be surprised if he had even tried to *come on* to Sister Agnes!

"It's okay," Malcolm said. "We all know about it. It's pretty hard to keep a secret in a town this size."

"The money is supposed to be divided up among all the women he's—you know," Hannah explained.

"How do we know who all that includes?" Rev. Wall asked, wishing for the first time in his life that he was a

Catholic priest instead of a Methodist minister. At least he'd know which Catholics had been to confession after their involvements. Life had taught him that in cases such as this, the women usually felt as guilty—or more guilty—than the men who had actually been the perpetrator.

"I suppose we could take an ad out in the Herald," Joe said, laughing. "Then we could sit back and wait to see who showed up. I wouldn't even charge for this one."

"That might be the only way to handle it," Malcolm said. "The paper's due out tomorrow morning?" he asked Joe.

"If I can get the blasted thing done," Joe said. "Sure is hard to get good help these days." He looked around, then said, "I'll get it out tomorrow if I have to stay up all night to do it."

Joe got to his feet and walked over to Malcolm, who was sitting at the head of the table. He leaned over and whispered something to him, then disappeared.

"Where's he going?" Hannah asked nervously.

Malcolm hedged a bit, clicking his fingernails on the table. "I suppose you've all heard about Bud Stryker by now."

The board members all nodded. Only Hannah and Tom Garborg acted surprised. Hannah'd been so busy running around to lawyer's offices and all she didn't know what had happened to Bud, but she was afraid to admit it. Tom had been God-knows-where, and he didn't have a clue what they were talking about.

"Guess he left somebody else in charge of the case while he's in the hospital."

Hannah assumed it was the FBI team. That was easy enough to handle. They didn't really seem all that competent.

"The FBI?" she asked timidly.

"No," Max Stryker said as she walked in with Joe and Rick. "They've got a lead on Paul Bunyan and Sally's whereabouts. They're hot on their trail."

Hannah gasped. "You mean *you're* on the case?" she asked Max.

"Yup," Max replied. "Got a problem with that?"

'Um, er, no, why would I?" Hannah asked. She hadn't expected this. Max Stryker was a newspaper reporter, pure and simple, yet Hannah sensed when Max and Bud had visited her that she had her father's instincts. Right now the only thing she had going for her was that nobody would blame her if she didn't really care if Bill ever came back or not. He didn't deserve any special favors, not by her or anyone else.

"Are they sure that's who's got Bill?" Joe asked. He still wasn't at all sure they were the guilty ones.

"They're pretty well convinced of it," Max said. "If they show up to collect the ransom money, guess that will cinch it."

"Aren't we forgetting one important thing?" Joe asked.

"What's that?" Malcolm asked.

"How do we know Bill is still alive? Whoever took him, if it was out of jealousy, like they think it is with Paul Bunyan—or rage, like it could be with any one of us—there aren't a whole lot of reasons to let the guy live."

With no warning, Hannah began to sob uncontrollably.

Max studied her. Was she really the grieving widow? Whoops. She reminded herself that nobody knew Bill was dead. Or did they? What about Mary? How big a role did she play in this whole theatrical production?

In a gesture of trying to comfort her, Max went over and stood beside Hannah, placing her hand on her shoulder.

"Don't worry, Hannah," she said calmly. "We'll get them. I promised Pops, and I can't go back on my word to him."

Max turned to Malcolm. "How long will it take you to get the money together?" she asked.

"About an hour, I would guess. Don't you think, Eric?"

What an ironic question, Max thought. She had never been convinced that Eric Hanson was capable of thinking at all. Not about this, or anything else.

"Sure," Eric answered. "I think I will check with Art, just to make sure what we are doing is legal."

"Good idea," Malcolm said. "Let's all meet back here in an hour then," he instructed the board.

Max and Rick left with Joe. They walked back towards the *Herald* office together, trying to fit the pieces of this crazy puzzle together.

"That Garborg guy sure didn't have much to say, did he?" Rick asked.

"Suppose Mary's right?" Max queried. "Maybe he does tie into it some way."

"How and why?" Joe asked. "What would he have to gain? He's an outsider."

"But Carol isn't," Max reminded him. "She got her start in business at the bank."

"Then there's still Sally and Paul Bunyan," Joe offered. "You think the FBI guys might be right?"

"Not on your life," Max said.

"Don't ask me," Rick said, shrugging his shoulders and grinning at them. "I just work here, remember? I'm just a computer junkie."

They all laughed, in spite of the tension that seemed to fill the whole town. It felt good, Max thought. She was glad she had friends.

"You want us to help with the paper?" Max asked Joe.

"I'll keep Rick here," he said, "but you'd better keep after this thing if you're going to keep your word to Bud."

"Pops!" Max yelled. "I'd better call Twin Valley and see how he is. Mind if I borrow your phone, Joe? I can have it billed to the house."

"Go ahead," Joe said, looking at her tenderly. Ever since Max first started working at the *Herald* when she was in high school, he had thought of her as the daughter he and his wife had wanted so desperately years ago. "This one's on me," he offered.

When she hung the phone up, Max's shoulders pulled in tight around her. She looked like she had the weight of the world on her.

"What is it?" Joe asked. "Is Bud...okay?"

"Mom says he's stabilized as good as can be expected, but they are going to have to do a triple bypass. That means he's going to be there quite a while."

"So you want to finish this thing up before they operate?" Joe asked, as if he could read her thoughts.

"Yeah," Max said. "That gives us about twenty hours."

"Bye," Joe said, pushing her out the door. "You've got work to do."

Catching Max completely off-guard, Rick came over and embraced her warmly. "You sure you'll be okay alone?"

Max laughed. "I don't think they want to kidnap me," she said. "I'll be fine." *But thanks for the concern*, she thought. She hadn't felt so secure in years. Maybe never.

"See you later," she said, getting into her car and squealing the tires as she drove away.

****

"What did you tell Pops about Hannah's phone call?" she asked Dick Barnes when she got to the phone company.

"I don't know that I should tell you," he said, winking at her. "It might be an invasion of privacy or something."

"The night you took me to the senior prom," Max reminded him, "you weren't too worried about invading *my* privacy!"

His face turned red. There was a time when they had been a *hot item*, but then she had gone off to the cities, he had gone to junior college, come home to run the phone company when his dad retired, and married Jeannie. No point in wondering now what might have been.

"I'm acting on Pops' behalf," Max said. "You heard about him, didn't you?"

"Yeah," Dick said. "I'm really sorry. He's a good man."

"Even the night he met you at the door with the shotgun because you didn't bring me home until four o'clock?" Max asked, her eyes sparkling as she teased him.

"Yeah," Dick said. "I guess if it had been my daughter I'd have felt the same way. He never did believe the radiator overheated, did he?"

"Not for a minute," Max said. "He said even if it had, it would have cooled off long before four a.m."

"Not as hot as it was that night," Dick said.

"The hottest thing that night was you!" Max taunted.

"You wanted to know about Hannah's phone call?" Dick asked, anxious to change the subject for fear Jeannie might walk in on them. "Okay, you win."

He went to the computer, punched in several numbers, waited while it click-click-clicked the message out on paper, which he tore off and handed to Max.

She studied the message, giving it a puzzled look, then asked, "What did Pops say about this?"

"Not much," Dick said. "If I remember right, it was something like, 'Hmmm! Interesting! Uh-huh!' That was about it."

"Can I take this with me?" she asked, folding the paper up and sticking it in her jeans pocket before he could answer.

"Be my guest," Dick said as he watched her leave. *She still has an awful cute wiggle when she walks*, he mused.

"Thanks," she called back to him, waving. "If this means what I think it does, you might be a real hero!"

CHAPTER FIFTEEN

Max drove home, but resisted the temptation to go inside. She sat, her head buried in her hands, running over all the events of the past few days. Her emotions ran the gamut, from guilt over Pops' heart attack to frustration on this stupid kidnapping case to the sense of security that had flowed over her when Rick so unexpectedly hugged her.

She looked up, staring at the house. It seemed so empty and foreboding. Eventually, she would have to go in, but for now the car offered the safety of a security blanket.

"I have to figure this thing out," she said aloud. "The answer has to be hidden here somewhere."

Her mind whirred around, trying to sort out all of the facts that she had at her disposal from the investigation. Bill Crane disappeared early in the morning, long before anyone would notice any activity at the bank. Sally was the first one at the bank after the kidnapping. The ransom note was obviously typed on one of the bank's own computers. Hannah claimed somebody had made a phone call asking Bill to go to the bank. She said she didn't recognize the voice, but no one had seen any strangers in town. Oh, she thought, except the FBI goons, but they arrived long after the fact. So, too, had Tom Garborg. Mrs. Kindred had narrowed the style of writing down to fourteen people. Then there was Paul Bunyan. Tom Garborg had been gone most of the day, and when he returned he had mud on his shoes. And

Mary had tried to play private eye all by herself; and she felt excluded because she had never been propositioned by the now infamous Bill Crane. Most of the rest of the women in Willow Creek would kill to be in that position. Maybe one of them did.

The facts all seemed to point right to Sally and Paul Bunyan. If she was sensible, she would help the FBI find them. Was it possible that the FBI guys were right? Was it really Sally and Paul Bunyan? She wondered if they had found them yet. They did claim to have a lead on their location. She and Pops had the same gut feeling about them. Were they that wrong? Well, if it was them, they would no doubt be brought in before long.

"Hannah." The sound of Pops' final word to her echoed in her ears, pounding, again and again, like a judge's gavel trying to bring order out of chaos.

"What did you mean, Pops?" she asked, then took out his black book and began to read. "What about her? Come on, talk to me."

Max turned the key in the ignition. The motor purred quietly. The heater spit its warmth in her face, causing it to take on a reddish hue—without even blushing.

She drove to the bushes near the Crane house, where Pops had parked out of sight while they visited Hannah. She killed the engine and sat, waiting, watching for Hannah to return from the meeting at the bank. They were still talking when Max left, but surely by now it must be over.

She reflected on the life Hannah and Bill Crane must have endured. Everybody in town knew about Bill's carryings on with all the women. Hannah couldn't be so naive that she wasn't aware of it too. Was she genuinely upset by Bill's disappearance? If Bill Crane was Max's husband, she would be downright glad to be rid of him. It was more than justifiable; it was almost funny. Like God had somehow finally gotten His revenge on the old goat.

"How sweet it is!" Max said, her speech taking on a near-perfect imitation of Jackie Gleason.

A sudden idea flitted across her brain, so quickly that she gazed up at the sky to see if there was a message written in lights somewhere above her.

What if Bill Crane faked his own kidnapping? She had heard of such things, but it was usually because they needed money. From the sounds of the board meeting, that was most unlikely. Then what purpose could such a scheme have?

Maybe he was sick. Even dying. He finally wanted to right the wrongs of his life. But he wasn't stupid! No, he would never openly admit his pursuits. If he could arrange for the money to be given to the women he had wronged—or at least attempted to taint—he could end his life with a clear conscience.

Suicide! Was Bill Crane lying in some dark, remote area of the forest? Was he wounded? Dead? Nobody would have the foggiest idea of where to look for his body.

Abelgaard! Bill's faithful Saint Bernard. If anybody could find Bill, it would be Abelgaard.

Try as she might, Max couldn't remember seeing the big old lazy dog when they had questioned Hannah. Did Bill take the dog with him?

Lost in her own deep thoughts, Max didn't see Dick standing outside the car until he tapped on the window. She jumped instinctively, then hopped out to see what he wanted.

"I've been looking all over for you," he said.

Max grinned. "We've got to quit meeting like this," she teased. "People might think we still have something going on."

"Not a chance," Dick said, returning her grin. "I'm going to be a daddy again."

"Congratulations!" Max said, suddenly realizing how much she was missing in the life of solitude she had chosen. "Is that what you came to tell me?"

"No, silly," he said. "I finally tracked down the operator who talked to Hannah when she made that phone call the morning Bill disappeared."

They stood, looking at each other. *He is still handsome, in a little-boy sort of way,* Max thought. She could have done worse.

She shook her head, trying to clear it.

"So?"

"She said..." Dick said, speaking so low she had to strain to hear him.

"Are you sure?" Max asked.

"She was positive," Dick insisted. "She thought it was funny at the time."

"Come on," Max said, grabbing Dick by the hand and pulling him along behind her as she ran towards the Cranes' house. "Do you want a little excitement?"

"Sure," he said, "but what..."

"Don't ask questions, just come on. I'll give you your first lesson in police work."

"But it might be dangerous," Dick said between gasps for air. He could have handled this a lot easier a few years ago, when he was used to being pummeled on the football field. He didn't realize how out-of-shape he was.

"Remember, I'm going to be a daddy," he reminded her.

"I'll protect you," Max said, laughing at the irony of the situation. Dick was at least twice her size. But, she was a woman of her word; she would make sure *Daddy* got home safe and sound.

"Shh!" Max commanded Dick as she pulled him down into the bushes in front of the Crane house.

"Ouch!" he yelped as he jumped up, rubbing his posterior where the prickly branches had stuck him.

"I said to be quiet!" Max repeated, trying not to laugh at him. She always knew men were such big babies; Dick just proved it.

"What are we looking for?" he asked in a coarse whisper.

"If my hunch is right, Hannah is going to come sneaking out of here pretty quick."

"Why?" Dick asked.

"Simple," Max answered. "She wants the money."

"The ransom money?" Dick asked, perplexed.

"Sure. After all, if Bill really did want the women he hurt to have it, she should be first in line. I don't know anybody who has suffered more—thanks to Bill Crane—than Hannah."

"I can't imagine she would do that," Dick confided. "She acts like she wants him back."

"Yeah," Max grumbled, "dead or alive!"

"You think Bill's dead?"

"Who knows?" Max said, shrugging her shoulders. "It's a possibility." Mary's words at the bank haunted her thoughts.

"I suppose anything's a possibility," Dick admitted.

"At least until we find him," Max agreed.

Rick came strolling up the street, whistling as he walked. He headed straight for the door at the Crane house.

"Psst!" Max said, waving at him to join them.

"What are you doing over here?" he asked. "And why is *he* here?"

Dick's presence had never bothered Rick before. In fact, he rather liked the guy. But he had never seen him in such close confines with Max before. He had heard that they used to be an "item."

"You turning into another Bill Crane?" he asked, a barb all-too-evident in his voice. "If my memory serves me right, you are a married man too." He turned his eyes to Max. "And I've heard tell you two have a history."

"Grrr!" Dick growled. "The green claws of jealousy are on the prowl again!"

"I'm not jealous!" Rick insisted. "Just answer my question. What are you two doing here?"

"Waiting for Hannah," Max replied.

Rick waited for her to elaborate. When she didn't, he asked, "And that's supposed to make sense to me?"

"Sure," Max explained. "It's simple. As long as *whoever* kidnapped Bill, Hannah is going to take advantage of the situation and get her hands on the money."

"But who dragged Bill off?" Rick and Dick asked, almost in unison.

Max laughed. "You two sound like a perfect pair for a sitcom: Rick and Dick, the Columbo twins! Have a little patience." Anything further she might have said was put on hold when they heard the Crane's back door open.

"What the..." Max asked, nearly getting knocked off her feet in the crouch position she had assumed to avoid being seen.

Abelgaard charged right past them, down the road as fast as his overweight, arthritis-ridden legs could carry him.

"Where's he going?" Rick asked. "I didn't think the old hound could move that fast."

"Let's find out," Max said, heading for her car. She jumped into the front seat and had the engine already revved up by the time the two men slammed their doors shut.

None of the trio was aware of Tom Garborg, who had been crouched down behind the bushes on the other side of the house. He wanted to follow them, too, but was afraid of being seen. Had Carol been right? Was Hannah Crane guilty of kidnapping her own husband? The scum! Even if she did it, or maybe *especially* if she did it, he didn't deserve any better. All he'd heard ever since he arrived in Willow Creek was how Bill Crane finally got what he deserved. And that was from the people who thought he'd been killed! No, there was no sympathy wasted on Bill Crane.

Max soon caught up with Abelgaard and followed him. He seemed to have a purpose, a mission. He headed directly for the alley behind the bank. He grabbed a rope that hung over the side of the huge dumpster, like he knew exactly what to do—step by step.

Max stopped the car, leaving the engine on so they could leave as soon as Abelgaard did.

The dog continued pulling until a black net, loaded with mountains of paper and trash, crashed to the ground. He pushed things aside with his big black nose until he found a cloth bag. He shook his head to free it from the other things it was caught on, then turned—the bag tightly clenched in his teeth—and ran towards the Crane house.

Max made a hurried U-turn and drove behind him. As they pulled up to the curb about a block away, she shut the car off. Rick and Dick opened their doors to get out.

"No!" she snapped. "Not yet."

"What?" Rick asked. "We've got her. She stole the money. Pure and simple. Or at least Abelgaard did. So let's go arrest the mutt."

"I told you," Max repeated, "not yet."

"I don't get it," Rick said.

"You sure would never make a good cop," Max chided.

"Or a P.I." Dick added.

"Oh, I don't know about that," Max said. "I'm sure he could do as good as those FBI geeks."

"Wonder if they've found Sally and Paul Bunyan yet?" Rick asked.

"It won't matter," Max said. "Not once we find out what Hannah's up to."

Before they knew it, Hannah Crane's car was speeding down the street. Max turned the car around again and followed her, close enough so she didn't lose her, but far enough behind that Hannah wouldn't spot her.

"Where do you suppose she's leading us?" Rick asked.

"With any luck, to..."

The car swerved as Max slammed on the brakes. To her surprise, when she looked in the rear view mirror she saw Abelgaard lumbering after them, as fast as he could, which wasn't all *that* fast. One good run in a day was enough!

"What's the matter?" Dick asked.

"Think somebody needs a ride," Max said, getting out and opening the back car door. "Come on, boy!" she called.

The huge creature climbed up onto the seat, laid his head—drool and all—on Rick's lap and closed his eyes.

****

As soon as he was sure it was safe, Tom Garborg pulled out in his big old Caddy and followed Max's car. With any luck he could hang back just enough to keep on their trail, yet remain invisible, even in that "boat."

CHAPTER SIXTEEN

Hannah's thoughts were running around in her head as fast as the tires on the car, which—according to the speedometer—was now rolling down the road at ninety miles an hour. She was as oblivious to the excessive speed as she was to the cars behind her. She had to get to the cabin. She never meant to hurt him. Just teach him a lesson. Maybe she was the one who needed the instructions. She had never been a spiteful person. She had certainly tolerated more than most women would have taken. But he had gone one step too far. He had to pay for his actions, and there was no one better than her who could give him the recompense he so deserved. As far as she was concerned, he had finally committed the unpardonable sin.

She turned the car onto the dirt road that cut into the deep, dark forest. By force, she slowed the car. Once again, she had to avoid the ditch. The ruts had frozen solid with the cold weather, and the light snow covered them, hiding them and making them far more treacherous in their seeming absence. When she reached the cabin, she sat alone in the car for nearly fifteen minutes. She wondered if he had survived the fall. She never meant to kill him; just teach him a lesson. Make him pay—with the fear for his life, not just his money—for what he had done to her. To her and so many other women from Willow Creek.

****

"Where does this lead?" Dick asked.

"I've seen it here before," Rick said, sitting on the edge of his seat in nervous anticipation. "The thrill of the chase" he had heard it called. If that's what this was, he wanted no part of it in the future. Abelgaard's body stretched in his unconscious sleep to follow Rick's lap as it moved forward. This was no thrill. This was downright sheer terror! Still, he crept even closer to the front, straining to see everything, not wanting to miss a single detail, even if he didn't fully comprehend what was happening.

"Looks like an old logging road," Max said.

"You don't know where we're going either?" Rick asked, fear filling his every word.

"Hopefully," Max said, "wherever it is it will lead us to Bill."

"You really do think Hannah kidnapped her own husband?" Dick asked.

"Either that," Max said, "or she figured out where he was apt to be hiding out."

"Hiding out?" Rick asked.

"As in *he rigged this whole thing himself*?" Dick asked. "But why?

"Maybe he needed the money for something, but he didn't want anyone to know about it, so he planned this whole thing himself," Max explained.

"But that doesn't make any sense," Rick said. "If he wrote the ransom note himself, he ordered the money to all be turned over to the women he'd been involved with over the years."

"Lots of things in life don't make sense," Max said. "Any other ideas?"

Rick scratched his head as he pondered the possible motives.

"Maybe he'd finally had a change of heart. Maybe he realized how terrible he was and he couldn't stand himself any more," Dick suggested.

"Or maybe he finally got caught," Rick added.

"Hey!" Max said, the car being drawn into a run and pulling it sideways as she turned to look at Rick. "You're starting to think like me!"

"That's dangerous!" Dick said, laughing. "So is taking your eyes off the road!"

"Don't worry, I'm in control," Max said.

"That's what I'm afraid of," Rick said, smiling at her. She was quite a lady! He had known her only a few short days, but he couldn't imagine life without her. As he pushed his thoughts back to *pre-Max* days, he realized it was almost impossible to remember what it had been like.

"Look!" Dick exclaimed, pointing off to the right of the road. "It's a cabin! Hannah is headed right towards it."

"It looks like she's got a gun!" Rick said nervously. "We'd better be careful."

"It isn't us she's after," Max said as she pulled off to the side of the road, well back from Hannah's car, and they watched and waited as she went inside.

****

Tom Garborg drove down the trail that led to Alex Broquist's place. He stopped, honked the horn one short blast and waited. In less than a minute Alex was opening the door and getting in.

"It's time?" Alex asked.

"I think so," Tom said. "I'm ready." He reached into his jacket pocket and pulled out a small pistol. Alex shuddered as he looked at it. He'd never liked guns for anything but hunting, but this was one hunt he was definitely ready for. The prey was for the abuse his mother had suffered all those years ago. Yes, for her he knew what he had to do.

"You remember how it works?" Tom asked.

"You bet," Alex said, taking the gun slowly and putting it into the pocket of his big buffalo-plaid jacket. "I'll wait until..."

"We can only hope and pray that he will come to, even if it is only for a few seconds. Unless, of course, he's already dead."

Alex shivered. It seemed odd to talk about prayer when you were thinking about... He'd never prayed much in his lifetime, and he'd sure never shot anybody before. If he was going to pray now, he thought he really should pray that he and Tom would be spared from having to take matters into their own hands. That was it; he would pray that Bill Crane was already dead. Somehow, that didn't seem right either.

****

As they got near the cabin, Tom stopped the car back a ways, and he and Alex got out of it and carefully sneaked around between the trees to the back of the cabin.

Tom looked inside and saw that Bill was there alone. He went inside and leaned over Bill's cold, still body. He felt for a pulse. It was faint, but it was still there.

Tom pulled at his gloves, making sure they were securely in place. He leaned over and picked up the rifle that was lying on the floor beside Bill. He carefully positioned his hands on it and squeezed the trigger so it appeared to have been fired.

In a flash, a bullet whizzed past Tom's head and Tom ran outside as fast as he could go. He went to a tree and sat down on the ground, pulling his stocking cap down over his face, and sobbed like a baby.

Alex stuck the pistol back into Tom's jacket pocket, then hurried through the woods to his shack. He went inside and unhooked the collar from around Cock-A-Doodle-Doo. He picked his companion up and stroked his feathers.

"Sorry I couldn't take you along," he said softly, "but that was nothing for you to see." Like he was a human being, he said, "I don't want you to have to tell anyone what I have done."

****

When she had finally gathered enough courage for the next step, Hannah walked up to the door and peeked inside. She saw Bill lying in the same pool of blood that had been there when she had left him earlier. She didn't stop to notice that some of the blood was dried, but on top of it was new, fresh blood.

"Bill!" Hannah screamed. "Bill! Wake up! I didn't mean it, honest!"

Hearing the shrieks from inside, all three of the *spies* jumped out and ran to the cabin, Abelgaard clomping behind them.

Rick arrived first. He flung the door open and they all charged inside. There, on the floor, was Hannah, with Bill's head cradled on her lap. She was sobbing violently. She was sitting in a pool of blood, which appeared to have been there for some time, and looked like it was frozen.

"Hannah!" Max cried out as she tried to pry her hands loose from Bill. "Is he..."

"Dead?" Hannah asked, still weeping. "No! He...he can't be!"

Dick leaned over them. He took Bill's hand in his, feeling for his pulse.

"He's alive," Dick said, "but we'd better get an ambulance out here—quick!"

"Always wondered why you had that silly phone in the car," Rick said, looking at Max, who had her hand on Hannah's shoulder comfortingly. "This is the perfect time to use it."

"I...I don't think it will work here," Max said, her face red with embarrassment. "It isn't set up for this frequency."

"That's no problem," Dick said. "I can jimmy-rig it to call the sheriff."

"Smart planning," Rick said to Max. "Who but you would think of bringing the head of the phone company along with us on a job like this?"

"Always knew he'd come in handy some day," Max said, winking at Dick.

In a flash, Dick was back. He silently said a word of thanks for the first-aid course he had taken several years ago. "Never know when it might come in handy," Old Doc Hammond had told them all. He wished his teacher was here now; he wasn't prepared for this. Not at all.

"The sheriff and the ambulance are both on their way," Dick said, breathing a huge heave of relief. "Let me have a look at him," he said, kneeling down beside Bill's big lifeless-looking body.

"Maybe we should untie him," Hannah said in a small voice.

In all the hubbub of the moment, no one had even noticed that his legs, stretched wide like a wishbone before it was broken, were tied to the table legs.

Max made a mental note of Hannah's remark. She wondered if she was just more observant than they were, or was she the one who had carefully wound the rope around Bill's ankles and then secured them to the two well-turned spindles that supported the antique round oak table?

Rick and Dick each reached for one of the ropes and began to free Bill.

"Don't know what difference it made to tie him up," Rick said. "The condition he's in, he couldn't have gotten very far, even if he had come to."

"Looks like somebody took a pretty good *whack* at his head," Dick said, turning back to study the lump that was swollen on the side of his forehead. "A couple of inches closer to his temple and he'd have bitten the dust."

"I didn't know if he'd come to or not," Hannah said solemnly. "If he did, and if he made it back to town, I knew he'd tell them..." Her voice drifted off into the unspeculated future she was facing.

Max stood up and pulled Hannah gently to her feet. She led her to the cold, crisp, black leather sofa.

"Maybe you'd like to tell us what happened before the sheriff gets here," she said. "If you do, we'll try to help you."

Hannah sat silently, her glazed-over eyes fixed on Bill's body. "Corpse," she said softly.

"He's not dead," Max said, putting her arm around her to comfort her. "Even if he was, there's not many people who would blame you."

"You all knew..." Hannah said.

"Everybody knew," Max admitted. "For years we've known."

"But not with Fran!" Hannah nearly shouted. "My own sister!"

They all looked at her in surprise. They knew he had tried to *make it* with every woman in town, but not Fran! Max tried no to laugh. If Bill Crane wanted to spread the word about his actions, the one sure way to do it was to hit on Fran. Everybody knew the one place nothing was sacred was in Fran's Beauty Shop, yet somehow she must have kept her tongue in her head when it came to her own life. If Maggie had heard about it, Max knew her mother would never have been able to keep that a secret.

"You mean Bill went after Fran?" Max asked.

"Yeah. Can you believe it? The worst part of it is that she gave in to him. I can never forgive them. Neither of them. Not my husband—with my own sister!"

Max tried to imagine the humiliation this venture must have caused her.

"All the other times," Hannah continued, "he never said anything to me. I guess he thought I was too stupid to figure it out. But people talk, you know."

"I know," Max said sympathetically.

"But this time he came home and actually bragged about his conquest! Can you imagine it?"

They all waited as she unfolded the story for them.

"I waited for a long time. More than a month. Then I did what I had to do. I got up early in the morning, long before he did. I waited for the phone to ring."

"The phone call," Rick said, recalling that Max had said somebody—whose voice Hannah claimed she didn't recognize—called the house and ordered Bill Crane to go to the bank.

"Yes," Hannah said. "I knew it would come."

"You had an accomplice?" Rick asked, trying to figure out who had placed the phone call to set the whole plan in motion.

"No," Hannah said. "I didn't need one. I figured it all by myself." In spite of the gravity of the situation at hand, she grinned—a sinister smile if ever there was one.

"I figured that one out," Max said. "With Dick's help. We checked your phone listing at the computer at the central office."

"And what did you learn?" Rick asked, feeling very much in the dark.

"It was really quite ingenious," Max said. "She called the phone company herself."

"But that wouldn't make *her* phone ring," Rick said, getting more confused with each passing second.

"No," Dick explained, "but she told the operator their phone didn't seem to be working, so she asked the operator to call her back to make sure it would ring."

"So the operator called back, making it seem like a *bona fide* phone call," Rick said.

"Brilliant!" Max said.

"Actually, it was," Hannah said almost proudly. "I thought I had it so well-planned even J.B. Fletcher couldn't have solved it. But I hadn't counted on you. You're better than her!"

"Thank you," Max said, smiling. No, she didn't blame Hannah for what she had done. It really was a good plan. If only something hadn't gone awry.

"I didn't mean to hurt him," Hannah said. "I just wanted to teach him a lesson. I went over to the bank by the back way and got there before he did. I know how slow he moves in the mornings. When he showed up, I made him type his own ransom note. I figured it was the least he could do. And I almost didn't have to worry about anything else. The thought of giving all of his hard-earned money away nearly killed him then and there."

They all waited for the rest of the story. Nobody interrupted. Nobody said a word. It was Hannah's turn.

"Then I made him get out in the car and come out here."

"What exactly is this place?" Rick asked. "How long has it been here?"

"Years," Hannah answered. "It was Bill's private hunting cabin. I don't know if anybody else has ever been here or not. Except Fran, of course. This is where he brought her. I don't think he remembered that I came out here to look at it before he bought it. That's when we were young—and in love..."

Max reached for Hannah's hand. She could see that this was hard for her, but she wasn't sure if the pain that showed on her face was from what she had done, or if it was the sheer memory of Bill's life that hurt.

"I took one of his hunting rifles to the bank with me," she said, pointing at the gun that lay at Bill's feet. "That's what really caused the whole problem. When I came out here to see if he was okay, he tried to pull the gun away from me."

She began to cry again. Hard. Uncontrollably. The tears rolled down her cheeks and onto her chest.

"He didn't know I never loaded it," she said when she was finally able to speak again. "He fell and hit his head on the edge of the table."

"That's how he hurt his head?" Max asked.

"Yes. I got scared. I started to run away. Then I thought about what would happen if he came to and got away. I couldn't let anybody else find him. I had to be the one. It had to be me."

"So you came back in and tied him up?" Rick asked.

"Yes," Hannah said. "I had tied him to the chair before, but I couldn't get him back up into it. He...was...so... heavy..." she said, as if she could feel the weight of his body all over again. As if she was reliving the horrible moment again, and again, and again.

"I knew when I got back to town I had to act fast. I didn't want him to die! I never wanted him to die!"

Her face was white and ashy at the thought of what might have been. What still could be. Max realized that if Bill Crane died, Hannah would be tried for murder, not just for kidnapping.

"There's only one thing I don't understand," Max said.

"What's that?" Hannah asked.

"Abelgaard," Max replied.

Hannah broke into loud guffaws. "He was the crowning touch. The *piece de resistance*," she said proudly.

"But when Pops and I were at your house," Max said, "I didn't see any sign of him anyplace."

"I know," Hannah said. "I had him down in the basement. If he got out by accident before the time was right, he would have ruined the whole thing."

Before she could continue, her mind flip-flopped back to Bill, who was still lying on the floor in front of them, leaving the rest of Abelgaard's part in the caper in limbo.

"What if he doesn't make it?" she asked again.

"I think he'll be all right," Dick said, trying to reassure her, "if the ambulance ever gets here."

Max glanced at her watch. It seemed like hours since they had arrived at this hidden haven, yet less than ten minutes had elapsed.

"I'm going out to call again. Maybe I can find out if they are on their way yet," Dick said.

"Let's go out and get some air, too," Max suggested, seeing that Hannah looked like she was about to faint. She sensed Hannah's hesitation and added, "There's nothing we can do for him until they come anyway."

Before Dick could reach Max's car, the sound of sirens blaring filled the silence of the forest air.

"This is it," Hannah said, standing up and holding her hands out in front of her. "Might as well put the handcuffs on."

"Oh, shoot!" Max said, smiling at her. It was a smile of pity, of support. A smile that gave Hannah the courage to face the future, whatever it held.

CHAPTER SEVENTEEN

The sheriff and two deputies arrived just in time to see the EMTs run into the cabin. Hannah followed them, but the medical workers barked, "Stay out of our way!"

"I have to make sure he's okay," she said, rushing on ahead.

"Don't do this," Max said, restraining her. "They can work much better if we all stay out here."

The sheriff and deputies went inside. Max strained to hear the low tones of their conversation, but she couldn't make out a single word.

The EMT came outside, his black bag in his hand. He walked over to the ambulance, threw it in the back door and climbed in the passenger side.

"What's going on?" Max demanded. "Why aren't you in there helping your partner?"

"No use," he said, shaking his head. "It's too late."

"But he was alive less than five minutes ago. What happened?"

"Pretty obvious," he said. "Don't play the fool with me."

"I don't have the foggiest idea what you're talking about," Max insisted. "He bled to death?"

"I suppose eventually," he said, "but the blood loss was obviously caused by the bullet in his brain."

Hannah collapsed on the ground. Max hurried to her side, yelling at the EMT who had just exited the cabin. "Get over here! Can't you see this woman needs medical attention? *Now!*"

"Coming," he said, hurrying to take charge of the situation. He bent over her, reaching for her hand to check her pulse. "Looks like she just passed out. Probably a mild case of shock. I'll take her in for observation."

"Not so fast," the sheriff said. "We've got a few unanswered questions here. In fact, we've got a ton of them."

"Can't that wait?" Max said, disgusted at their insensitivity. "You can see she's in no shape to answer anything right now."

"She's not the only one we need to question," the sheriff said. "It looks to me like you are all in cahoots on this thing. I don't want anybody leaving until I say so."

"Listen here, Mister!" Max said, her hands on her hips and her feet firmly planted about a foot apart. "I don't think you know who I am! Bud Stryker is my dad, and he put me in charge of this case. This whole thing started out in Willow Creek and I've been on it since the beginning. I don't want some outsider butting in on it now."

"You're Max?" the sheriff asked.

"Yeah," Max said. "So?"

"Bud has bragged about you ever since the first day I got here two years ago. Max this...Max that...Max can do no wrong...Max...Max...Max! But I'll be damned! Of all the things he said about Max Stryker, he forgot to mention one trivial little detail."

"And what's that?" Max asked.

"I just, um, assumed *Max* was his son. Whoever heard of a gal named Max?"

"Everybody in Willow Creek," Rick said, coming to Max's defense. "It's Maxine, for your information. Not that it makes any difference. Male or female, Max Stryker is the best!"

Max blushed. She wasn't used to having somebody else fight her battles. She could handle herself pretty well, and she didn't need his help. Still, it felt good to have him back her up. She'd thank him later—properly.

"Never mind that," Max said. "We are still trying to figure out what happened to Bill. It looks to me like one of you guys must have shot him. He was fine when we left him, and there hasn't been anybody else here except us and you. We were all inside at the same time. Nobody was alone with him at all. Not until you came."

When the EMTs were satisfied that Hannah was all right, they went inside and got Bill Crane's body. Just like on big time TV, the sheriff drew a chalk line around where the body had been. Max had stared at Bill lying there enough that she could remember exactly where and how he was without the help of extra measures. It was a picture she would never forget. She'd seen lots of dead bodies in her work in St. Paul covering the crime beat, but this was different. This wasn't just a body; it was somebody she knew. In spite of that, she couldn't feel any remorse at the loss of Bill Crane. By all rights, somebody should have gotten even with him years ago. But who on earth did it?

As she watched them carry Bill's body out, she thought of Pops. She wondered if they had done the operation yet, or if he was even stable enough so they could start it. As soon as she got out of here, she decided, she would head straight to the hospital in Twin Valley. This time, when Pops needed her, she was going to be there for him.

"Okay," the sheriff said, plopping down into the one easy chair in the room, "now let's get to the bottom of this. Whodunit?" He grinned at the play on words, so well-known to all real investigators. Like Pops, he had never handled a real live kidnapping case before either, let alone a murder! Wow! This was his big break. If he could find some way to take credit for this bust, he was a shoe-in for next year's election as sheriff. As it was, he had inherited the post. When the last sheriff died, it just sort of fell into his lap. He had been appointed by the county commissioners.

"I'm afraid I'm the guilty one," Hannah said, her head hanging down and her eyes fixing on the cracks in the boards on the floor.

"You?" the sheriff asked. "Why, pardon me, ma'am, but you don't look like you could hurt a flea. Sure not somebody the size of that guy they just hauled out of here."

"This helped," Hannah said, reaching over and grabbing the rifle.

"Hey, just a minute!" the sheriff shouted. "Don't shoot! You've got a bad enough rap going for you now."

"Don't worry," Max said. "It isn't loaded."

"Never has been," Hannah admitted. "I just used it for effect when I kidnapped him."

"You might have kidnapped him," the sheriff said, "but you couldn't have shot him with an empty gun."

"Shot him?" Hannah asked. "No, I didn't shoot him. You don't know what you're talking about. Nobody shot him."

"He's got a hole in his head," the sheriff said.

"Heck," Hannah said, "he got that when he hit his head on the table when he tried to grab the gun away from me. He didn't know the gun wasn't loaded."

"Nope," the sheriff argued, "there was a bullet hole as plain as the light of day in his head. Right through his forehead. Sure, there was a gash on the back of his head, but that isn't what killed him."

"I tell you," Hannah said, "I kidnapped him. Take me to jail and get it over with."

"Lady, you're crazy!" the sheriff said.

"Exactly!" Max shouted excitedly. "That's it! Don't you see? This poor woman has been married to Bill Crane for years and years. He drove Hannah to this point. He made her crazy. It's not her fault she did what she did. I think if you hear the whole story, Sheriff, you'll agree that that is exactly the point. She is crazy. Crazy from loving the man she married. When he betrayed her with her own sister, it was the last straw. The one that broke the camel's back. That's it, Sheriff. You can't hold her responsible for her actions. If any of the rest of us had lived that long with a louse like Bill Crane, we probably would have made sure the gun was loaded."

"She didn't know the gun was loaded." Dick began singing the old country western hit from a bygone era.

The sheriff shook his head. "Personally, I think you are *all* a little off."

"Well, okay," Hannah said, again holding her hands out in front of her. "Are you going to cuff me and haul me in?"

"I don't think that's necessary," the sheriff said. "Like I said, you don't look like you could hurt a flea."

"You never know what us wacky ones might do," Hannah said, laughing.

For a fleeting moment, the sheriff thought she might be right. Maybe she was more dangerous than she appeared. No, he was sure he could handle her. Him and his deputies. Still, he'd lock the rifle in the trunk of the squad car, just to be sure. No sense in taking unnecessary chances.

"We've still got a murder to solve," Max said. "We were all with Hannah every single minute. We will all testify that there is no way she could have killed him. So, we've still got a killer on the loose."

"Maybe he did himself in," the sheriff suggested.

Max laughed. "That's the craziest thing I ever heard. There's a *rifle* on the floor, not loaded, beside a guy that's completely unconscious! Even if it had been loaded and he'd have come to long enough to shoot himself, there's no way he could get his hand out far enough to shoot himself in the head with a long-barreled rifle!"

"Guess not," the sheriff said, shrugging. *If word of this gets out*, he thought, *you're sunk in the election!*

"Why don't you let me take custody of Hannah?" Max asked. "I will make sure she doesn't leave town."

"Where would I go?" Hannah asked, laughing.

"You sure?" the sheriff asked Max. "I think you're right; the old bat is loony."

"No problem," Max assured him. "Go on ahead. I'll wrap things up here."

"I'd better help," he said.

"It's okay," Max insisted. "If I need your help I'll call you." *In your mother's dreams,* she thought.

Max motioned to Rick and Dick to get in the car. She took Hannah by the arm and escorted her to the front door, then she went around and slid into the driver's seat.

She sat, waiting, for the sheriff and his deputies to leave. As they waited, Hannah turned to Max. "What tipped you off?" she asked.

"It was Abelgaard," Max confided. "I had almost everything figured out. Then when he came charging out of the house, we followed him. He led us right to the alley out behind the bank. We watched him retrieve the bag of money and take it back to you. Then you split. I mean, wow! You were really traveling! I could hardly keep up!"

Hannah grinned again. "I kept him locked in the basement during the day. At night I would take him over to the bank and show him how to pull on the rope I had tied to the net inside the dumpster. I put a nice juicy hamburger in the net, and when he managed to get it out I let him eat the hamburger for a reward. There's nothing Abelgaard likes better than a good juicy hamburger. When it was finally time—when the money was there—I turned him loose. He did just like he was supposed to. In a couple of minutes he was back with the bag full of money. By the way, here," she said, throwing her car keys to Max. "Make sure the girls get their fair share. The money's in the trunk."

"That reminds me," Hannah said, "where is the mutt?"

"Haven't seen him lately," Rick said. "Come on, Dick. Let's go dog- hunting."

"Don't shoot him!" Hannah shouted.

"Don't worry," Dick said. "We'll bring him back safe and sound." The two men scooted into the woods, Dick whistling for the dog and Rick calling his name.

"Be quiet!" Rick ordered. "I think I hear him." Off in the distance was the definite whine of a dog. They headed in that direction. When he came into view, he was licking the face of Tom Garborg, who was sitting on the ground, his back leaning against the trunk of a big jack pine tree.

"What the..." Rick asked. "What are you doing out here?"

"I...I'm not sure," Tom answered. "I just know I had to get out of there."

"Where?" Rick asked.

"That cabin. With all that blood. With that dead man. Was...that was Bill Crane, wasn't it?"

"Yeah," Rick said. It had never dawned on him that the new guy at the bank didn't even know what Bill Crane looked like. And why was he out there? What possible connection could there be between some stranger from St. Paul and a small-time hick bank president in Willow Creek? The only thing that popped into his mind was that Tom Garborg's wife, Carol, was a local gal, but she had left town several years ago. In fact, Rick had never even met Carol Garborg. It didn't make any sense. None of this made any sense. "How'd you know he was dead?"

"I...I saw all the blood," Tom repeated. "I just knew he was dead, I think."

"You knew?" Rick asked. "Or you thought?"

"I don't know," Tom said, rubbing his head like it ached like fury. "Will somebody take me home?"

Rick looked around. There was no sign of his car anywhere. "How did you get here?"

"I drove, I think," Tom said. It was obvious that he was confused. Apparently he wasn't used to dealing in gruesome affairs. Bankers weren't murderers. Crooks, yes, but murderers, no.

"Where is your car?" Dick asked.

"It's—someplace behind the bushes about a mile back from the cabin." He rubbed his head again. "Would one of you drive it home for me? I don't feel so good."

"In a minute," Rick said, "but we'd better get Abelgaard back to Max and Hannah. They will be worried."

Dick and Rick supported Tom as they began walking. Rick called back "Come on, boy" to Abelgaard, who obediently followed behind his heels.

As they emerged from the woods, Max ran towards them. "What's he doing here?"

"I don't know, exactly," Rick said. "I don't think he does, either. Abelgaard found him out in the woods, all scrunched down by a tree."

"Go on," Max said when he paused.

"It sounds like he saw Bill through the back window. Guess he got spooked and took off for the woods. I think he's in shock."

"So what do we do with him?" Max asked.

"Take him back to town, I guess," Rick said. "He wants one of us to drive him back in his car."

"I'll take him in," Dick said. "Where are your keys?"

"In my pocket here, I think," Tom said, reaching into his suit coat pocket. He held his keys in his hand, but in the process a small pistol caught on them and fell onto the ground at his feet. Max went to grab for it, but another hand got there first. One of the deputies had emerged from the cabin, which they had been checking out, just in time to see the gun.

"I'll take that," he said, picking it up with a Kleenex and dropping it into a plastic bag.

"Look what we've got here," he called to the sheriff.

The sheriff came over to join the group. "Well, I'll be. I'll bet you a five-spot that matches the bullet from the victim. Won't take long for them to figure that out in Duluth."

"Well, I guess that lets Hannah off the hook for the murder at least," Max said.

"But there are still the kidnapping charges," the sheriff said. "Are you sure you still want to take charge of her?"

"No problem," Max said. "Come on, Hannah. Let's get you back home. I think you've had enough for one day. Come on, Abelgaard." They both climbed into the back seat of Max's car. Max went around and got into the driver's seat and started the engine. She let out a long sigh. This had been quite a day for her, too.

Max backed the car up so she could turn around and head back to Willow Creek. She was jarred when she heard a knock on the front passenger window. She looked up to see Rick running along beside the car.

"What does a guy have to do to get a ride around here?" he asked, grinning.

"Stick your thumb out," she said. He obeyed, and she slammed the brakes on to let him in. They sat and waited as they watched the sheriff snap the handcuffs on Tom Garborg, load him in the squad car and pull out ahead of them. Dick followed them in Tom's car, then the deputy in Hannah's car joined in the procession and Max and the gang brought up the rear.

****

The FBI men, all six of them, piled out of the only police car Willow Creek owned. With Bud Stryker in the hospital, they had assumed the usage of the vehicle. Looking very much like the proverbial sardines in a tin can, they moved around, trying to regain use of their limbs. As if the fit wasn't tight enough with the six of them, they tugged and pulled on the other two passengers still inside.

"I'm telling you," Paul Bunyan shouted as he got out, "I didn't do it! And neither did my Sally!"

"They're quite right," the sheriff said, as he, too, got out of his own squad car. "We have the guilty party right here, complete with the weapon and all."

"But who…" Hannah said as she hopped out of the car, appearing as free as a bird. "I kidnapped him. And I'd do it all over again, if I had the chance."

"Mrs. Crane?" Frank asked in surprise.

"The very same," she said, again almost proud of her accomplishment. "He had it coming to him, but I suppose somebody as smart as you had that all figured out."

"Of course," Frank said. "But why?"

"Why not?" Hannah asked. "But I didn't know Tom Garborg was going to show up to finish what I started. Now, ready to take my statement?" she asked the sheriff.

"Whenever you are," he said, leading her into Bud Stryker's office. "And like Max said, I'm sure any jury in these parts would buy your plea of insanity, hands down. So, I will recommend to the judge that he release you on your own recognizance."

"Thanks," she said, standing on her tiptoes and giving the sheriff a light peck on the cheek. "I'm glad it's finally over."

"But where's Bill Crane?" Frank asked.

"Dead," Max said simply.

"She killed him?" Frank asked, surprised.

"Heck no," Max said. "She already told you that Tom Garborg did it."

"The bank officer?" Frank asked.

"Yup," Max said. "And don't ask me why. I haven't got that figured out yet. But give me a little time and I will. The way I see it, your work here is about over. You might as well pack up your bags and head back to Washington."

"Won't be too soon for me," Frank said. "I just hope the boss sees it that way, too."

"I'll make sure he does," Max said under her breath.

****

Max dropped Rick and Dick off at the *Herald* office, then drove on to Twin Valley to see how Pops was faring.

She hurried to his room, expecting to find both him and her mother there.

"Where's Pops?" she frantically asked the nurse.

"Mr. Stryker?" the nurse asked. "He's out of surgery. Your mother is down in the recovery lounge, waiting for him to wake up."

"Is he okay?" Max asked, almost afraid to vocalize the question.

"He should be just fine," the nurse assured her. "The doctor said everything went great."

Max hurried to the recovery room to find her mother.

"You can go in," the attendant told Maggie just as Max arrived. "He's asking for you."

"Oh, Mom!" Max said, giving her mother an unexpected hug. "I'm sorry I wasn't here again."

A tear glistened in the corner of her eye. She hadn't meant for it to be this way. Not again. She had failed them with his first heart attack, and now she had done it again.

"Did you get the bad guys?" Maggie asked.

"Both of them," Max replied.

"Both?" Maggie asked.

"Hannah," Max said, "and Tom Garborg. Come on, I'll tell you and Pops at the same time. They said he's asking for us."

They walked into the recovery room, hand in hand. Bud was pale and he looked tired, but he was alive. His heart was repaired, giving him a new lease on life.

"Did you get her?" he asked Max.

"Hannah?" Max said.

He nodded.

"She's with the sheriff now. I think she'll get off with a plea of insanity."

Bud laughed. "She's about the sanest person I know."

"Hush!" Max warned him. "Don't let anybody hear you say that. You'll blow her whole defense."

"Wouldn't want to do that now, would we?" Bud asked. "You done good, kid. So they found Bill?"

"Bill's dead," Max said.

"What?" Bud asked. "But how?"

"Don't get too excited," Maggie warned. "Maxine will tell you all about it."

"He was shot," Max said, "but Hannah didn't do it. Tom Garborg did."

"Tom Garborg?" Bud asked. "Why the hell..."

"We have to figure that one out yet. The sheriff's got Tom in custody. He's, well, in a state of shock."

Maggie stood back a little ways, watching her husband and her daughter interact. *Like father like daughter*, she thought, smiling at them. She felt like the luckiest woman in the whole wide world.

"Come here, woman!" Bud ordered as gruffly as his weak voice would allow. "Got a kiss for your old man?"

Maggie bent over him and kissed him gently on the lips, right through the plastic tube that stuck out of his mouth. "You done good, too, kid."

"Gonna keep me around a while yet?" he asked, the twinkle still in his eyes.

"You betcha," Maggie said. "After all, we've got a trial or two to attend. I understand invitations are already out."

"I want to hear the rest of the story," he said. "Don't leave out one gory little detail."

"Later," Max said. "For now, get some rest. You'll have plenty of time. Seems to me you aren't going anyplace real soon."

In spite of his anxiety to hear all about it, his eyes were soon closed and he slept.

Maggie and Max waited together until the doctor came and said, "He seems to be fine. We are moving him back up to his own room."

They went ahead so they would be there to greet him when he arrived. When he finally woke up, he looked up at the two women in his life, one on each side of him. He didn't know how he had been so lucky. Of course he had been a better man than Bill Crane. He reached up, slowly, and took each of them by the hand.

"You're a good woman, Maggie Stryker," he said smiling at her. Tears of gratitude filled her eyes.

"And you," he said, winking playfully at Max, "I'm proud of you. I couldn't have done a better job myself."

"I had a little help," Max admitted.

"Rick?" Bud asked, a knowing glint in his eyes.

"Yes," Max said slightly. "Which reminds me, I'd better head back home. We do still have a newspaper to put out. I'll bet Joe is ready to fire me, and I've hardly started working yet. They'll never make it if I don't get back to help them."

"Yeah, sure," Pops said. "Like the whole time you were gone there wasn't one single issue of the *Herald* that ever got out on time! Sure there isn't another reason you're in a hurry?"

Max realized all of a sudden that there was another reason. *Rick.* Her mind raced back to the few moments she had spent in his arms. It was a feeling of security and safety she had never experienced before. *Not even with Dick*, she thought. It felt good.

"None whatsoever," she said, trying to sound convincing.

"You two were pretty good together," Pops said. "You ought to try for a repeat performance."

"Right," Max said. "Like there is so much exciting going on in Willow Creek. That was a once-in-a-lifetime thing, believe me."

She turned and walked away. "I'll be back first thing in the morning," she called back to them. "You're staying overnight, Mom?" she asked.

"Yes," Maggie said. "I've got a room upstairs. You know, where they let the intruders spend the night."

"Okay," Max said. "Take it easy, Pops."

A crowd of reporters stood in the lobby, waiting for Max to come down from Bud's room. She was already a local hero. Whether it was for cracking the case, or for making sure that Bill Crane was truly dead—which the reporters were convinced she had had a part in—was questionable.

Max scrunched down, pulling the hood on her jacket up around her face. She was used to being on the other end of the microphone. After all, she was a reporter. First and foremost, she was a reporter, not a private eye.

Her mind quickly passed over all the questions she would ask if she was them and somebody else—*anybody else*—was her. Before she could formulate a game plan, the questions began to fly.

"What gave you the first clue that Mrs. Crane was the guilty party?"

"How well did you know the victim?"

"Did he ever come on to you?"

"Are you sorry—or relieved—that he is dead?"

"Is your father's heart attack a result of the investigation?"

"Who is this Rick guy? Are you romantically involved with him?"

"Is that big guy really named Paul Bunyan?"

"How much input did the FBI have in this case?"

Max stuck her hand up in the air. "I have no comment now," she said. "I will try to get the people involved together by tomorrow and we will hold a press conference back in Willow Creek. That's all for now."

She made a mad dash for her car. It was not to avoid the cold wind that blew the snow around that caused her to hurry, nor even the group to which she had belonged just a week ago. No, it was what—or who—was waiting for her back in Willow Creek.

She glanced around and spotted the TV News van, which sported the big bold letters *CNN*. She had assumed they were from the TV station in Hibbing, or at the best Duluth. So she had made it to the big time. She could have worked at the paper in St. Paul for the rest of her life and she would never have gotten where she was right now. She wondered if she should ask them for a job after the press conference she had promised them.

"We were pretty good together," she said aloud as she drove out of the hospital parking lot, "but there isn't likely to be something so dramatic as a kidnapping to put us together again." She turned the radio on and began to hum to the strains of "Love Me Tender" on the oldie station.

****

Max stopped at Bud's office. There was a note on the desk. She picked it up and read, "Max: We are on our way back to big-time crime. The big boss wanted us to stay until it was all wrapped up, but I convinced him Max Stryker could handle anything. If you need anything, call me. Frank. P.S. The big boss thinks 'Max' is a guy, so try to disguise your voice if you ever talk to him. I didn't want him to know I'd been outsmarted by a woman."

Max smiled as she stuffed the note in her back pocket. She had to get to the *Herald*. Joe and Rick needed her.

CHAPTER EIGHTEEN

Max tried to entice Rick to join her for the press conference. "You were part of the whole thing," she argued. "They are curious about you. They want to talk to you."

"They want to crucify me!" he insisted. "I'm not used to being in the spotlight. You will handle it just fine. Besides, go find the FBI guys. They'll love looking like they made the case. Who's to know they were chasing the wrong guys the whole time? They will want to be there to set the record straight. At least straight in their eyes."

"Frank left a note for me in Pops' office," Max said. "Seems they've skipped town. Guess they wanted to save face in case the reporters asked the wrong questions. This will be all over the country, you know. It's the crew from CNN that wants the meeting, not some local yokel who doesn't matter."

"Wow!" Rick said, letting out a long, low whistle. "So you are going to be famous! By tomorrow night you won't even know who I am."

"Fat chance!" Max sputtered. "By tomorrow night they will all be gone, and if I know the press, the big bosses will scrap the whole thing. People like Ted Turner don't give a hoot about what happens in a little joint like Willow Creek, Minnesota."

"We'll see," Rick said.

****

At ten o'clock sharp, Max Stryker walked out from a side door to the platform at the high school gym. It was the only place that was big enough to hold everybody who had come for the show.

Max gulped as she looked around. Everybody in Willow Creek was there. There were reporters from all across the country: *New York Times, Chicago Sun, Minneapolis Herald-Tribune, Good Morning America, Today Show,* of course lots of regional newspapers and TV stations, the original culprits from *CNN,* and over in the corner even a couple from the *National Enquirer.*

Max smiled back at a young woman she recognized wearing a tag marked "Minneapolis Herald-Tribune." At least one of her cohorts from her old beat in the now-defunct St. Paul *Pioneer Press* had managed to snag a job at the "big one." More power to her!

Max adjusted the microphone on the podium in front of her. She was glad for the protection the big wood mass provided her; she never knew her knees could shake like this. *Good exercise,* she thought, smiling. She flipped the switch to the "On" position and nodded her head, giving the signal that she was ready to get the show on the road.

Voices flew at her from all over. She raised her hand and said simply, "One at a time, please."

"Did you ever have an affair with the victim?" came the first question.

Max cringed. She didn't want to go there. She would have to try to shift the questions in another direction as soon as she could.

"I doubt that any of the women in Willow Creek had an actual affair with Mr. Crane, although I have to admit that it probably wasn't because he didn't try."

"So he did *come on to* you?"

"That is not material for this interview. If this is the direction you continue to pursue, it will be a very short session."

She turned and started to leave.

"Is Mrs. Crane really insane?"

Feeling an obligation to come to Hannah's defense, Max returned to the podium.

"I am not a psychiatrist, but in my opinion, she was at least acting under extreme duress. In that respect, she may be *unbalanced*. But again, I am not qualified to answer that question."

"Is there really a guy named Paul Bunyan who was a prime suspect?"

"Everybody calls him Paul Bunyan," Max replied. "His real name is John Martin, but he is a very large lumberjack. Thus the name, Paul Bunyan."

"Where are the FBI? I heard they were called in on the case."

"They have already left town. Yes, because of the nature of the crime—kidnapping is a federal offense, you know—they were called to come and assist in the investigation."

"We heard they were chasing the wrong suspects."

"In a case such as this, almost everyone is a suspect. They were just following the clues they had."

"So you were pleased with the way they worked?"

"No comment." She knew they couldn't get her for liable with this one, but the message of a restraint such as this answered the question as loudly as actual words.

"We understand your father, the chief of police, is in the hospital after having had open heart surgery. Was the case too much for him to handle? Is he planning to turn his job over to you?"

"My father is perfectly capable of handling anything that comes his way. He has had some heart problems recently; it is genetic. It has nothing to do with his ability—or lack of it. And no, I have no intention of replacing him. I am, like you, a reporter. I came home to help with the local newspaper because the owner and publisher is retiring."

"Who is this Rick character you seemed to be with all the time?"

"Rick is a fellow employee at the newspaper."

"Are you two romantically involved?"

"We are fellow employees."

"And romantically involved?"

"Next question," Max snapped, pointing to her friend from Minneapolis.

"How did you know Mrs. Crane was the kidnapper?" she asked.

"She had the most to gain, or to lose, by the actions of Bill Crane. It was a simple matter of deduction and elimination."

"What do you predict will happen to Mrs. Crane and Tom Garborg?"

"That is up to a jury."

"What was Tom Garborg's interest in all this?"

"I have no idea."

"Does he have a connection to Willow Creek?"

Max hesitated. She knew Carol was due to have her baby any day now. They didn't need this at such a time.

"I do not know of any connection between Tom Garborg and the victim."

She breathed a sigh of relief when the next question was "Are you glad that Bill Crane is dead?"

"Murder is a serious crime. No one should have to endure it. I, like my father, believe in the justice system. I just hope and pray that justice will be done, in this case like in any other."

Max turned and walked away, disappearing into the side room off the platform. She hurried to lock the door. She had seen some of these interviews before. She had even been a part of them—on the other side. She knew how persistent and ruthless they could be.

She waited for several minutes, afraid of the sound at the door. Finally, it came, but it was one lone knock, not the sound of a riotous, bloodthirsty crowd.

"Who is it?" she asked cautiously.

"It's me," came the familiar, welcome voice. "Rick."

She unlocked the door and let him in. She had never seen a more welcome face.

"You handled them like a pro," he said, smiling proudly at her. "Your Pops will be proud of you too."

She returned the smile. She caught the "too." He wasn't admitting that he was proud of her. Not exactly. But close enough.

****

"Are you sure you want to do this?" Carol Garborg's mother asked her the day of the trial. "You know it's going to be hard on you—no matter what happens."

"I have to go," Carol said, kissing little Michael goodbye. "Thanks so much for watching Michael for me." She saw the uneasy look in her mother's eyes. "Tom needs me, now more than ever." She paused momentarily. "I believe in him. I know you'd do the same for Dad."

"Your dad would never kill anybody," her mother reminded her.

"Yeah, right, Mom," Carol said as she slammed the door. She could at least pretend to be a little bit sympathetic.

She sure hoped Max and Art Moore could manage this. They had been successful with Hannah; she was free as a bird on a plea of temporary insanity. Would they be able to pull the same scam with Tom? Their plan of going for temporary amnesia was pure brilliance. They all knew Tom was as guilty as hell. The only thing he had going for him was that they couldn't find one single witness who didn't wish—a hundred times over—that Bill Crane was dead.

****

Inside the big old St. Louis County courthouse in Duluth, Max, Bud, Rick, Joe and Art Moore were gathered in a huddle. They had their strategy all worked out. With any luck at all, Tom would cooperate to the fullest, even when his subconscious was being questioned.

"Here comes the goon squad!" Max commented as she saw Frank and his men meander down the hall. "Who invited them?"

"I did," Bud said. "They are witnesses, you know. And, after I talked to Frank on the phone last week, I felt they could help us."

"Whatever," Max said, shrugging her shoulders. She knew better than to argue with Pops.

"Good luck, man," Ed Pomeroy, the dashing young prosecutor, said as he walked up to Art Moore on his way into the courtroom.

Max snickered. If he was waiting for a similar response, he was in for a surprise. It was, she knew, his first trial. Poor guy! He didn't stand a chance of winning. Still, his comment made Max wonder if he had some history with Bill Crane too.

"We'd better go on in," Art said to his cohorts. "It's almost time."

Bud held back a little, reaching for Max's hand.

"You done good, kid!" he said, brimming with pride.

"Thanks, Pops," Max said, pleased with his approval. "You think we can do it?"

"You bet we can!" he said confidently. "We're Strykers!"

It was enough. Max was ready to take on the world. Pops was right, as usual. They had done their job well, and this trial was bound to pay off big-time when Tom Garborg was found "Not guilty."

"The Honorable Judge Deborah Hill presiding," the bailiff said.

"Wow!" Max said softly. "We really lucked out on this one. No way some woman judge is going to feel sorry for old Bill Crane and what he did to nearly every woman in Willow Creek."

Rick, who was sitting beside her, reached over and gently squeezed her hand. "Mom would be proud of us, too," he said quietly.

The witnesses were called to the stand, one by one, by Mr. Pomeroy. In less than an hour he announced, "The prosecution rests, your honor." He then returned to his seat and waited for Art Moore to do his thing.

One by one, Art called *character witnesses* to the stand. After five of the people who had been affronted by Bill Crane in the past, Judge Hill called both attorneys to the bench.

"This is all very interesting," she said, "but what does this have to do with the case?"

"They are character witnesses," Art said.

"But they are all attesting to the character of the victim. He's not on trial here. Get on with the show!"

"Yes, your honor," Art said. Turning away from her, he surprised everyone by announcing, "I call Mary Bertheson to the stand." A deadly hush fell over the room.

"I do," Mary answered the bailiff as he swore her in.

"How long did you know Bill Crane?" Art asked.

"I guess almost all my life," Mary said.

"And did you like him?" Art asked.

"He was...okay," Mary responded.

"How old were you when you began working at the bank?"

"Sixteen," Mary answered.

"And how did Bill Crane treat you?"

"I...I don't know what you mean," Mary said, all three-hundred-plus pounds squirming nervously in the chair.

"Did he show you respect?"

"He...he told me many times that I was doing a good job," Mary said, looking down at the floor.

"Did he treat you the same way he did the other girls?"

"Objection," Ed Pomeroy shouted. "This is irrelevant."

"Objection overruled," Judge Hill said. "Continue, Mr. Moore. But please get to the point."

"Answer the question."

"He...he never bothered me," Mary said, still not looking up.

"What do you mean by *bother*?" Art asked.

"He...um...he never came on to me, if that's what you mean."

"Did he come on to the other girls at the bank?" Art asked.

"Most of them," Mary said. "I think all of them, probably. I know he did to Sally. And Karyn. And..."

"Move to strike, your honor," Ed Pomeroy interrupted. "Hearsay."

"Sustained," Judge Hill said, giving Art a stern warning look.

"Did you ever *see* him make an advance on anyone?" Art asked, rephrasing the same question.

"Well, there was the time I caught him in the vault with Karyn."

The crowd whispered, their eyes all fixed on Karyn.

"What were they doing?" Art asked.

"He, um, he had his pants open," Mary said, her face bright red by this time.

"And what was Karyn doing?"

"He had her pinned against the wall, but she was hitting him as hard as she could. When I came in, he didn't even apologize for what he was doing. He just zipped his pants up and walked out. Karyn went home for the rest of the day."

"But Bill Crane never made an advance to you?" Art asked.

"No," she replied simply.

"How did that make you feel?"

"Objection!" Ed Pomeroy yelled.

"Overruled," Judge Hill said. "Please answer the question."

"It made me mad!" Mary said, her voice full of the anger she felt. "He tried to get everybody in the bank. Everybody but me! I was the best worker he had, but he never paid any attention to me. No, I wasn't good enough for him! Good old Mary! She's a damn good worker, but that's all she's good for. Do you know how it felt when everybody else was griping about how he acted, I couldn't say a word? Not one. Why? Because I wasn't even good enough—not even for old Bill Crane! I could have killed him!"

"Order!" Judge Hill bellowed, pounding her gavel on the desk to try to regain order in the courtroom.

Art Moore turned to the observers. "It seems that *everyone* wanted Bill Crane dead." He turned back to Mary. "You may step down," he said.

"If it please the court," he said, changing his strategy once his point was made—most effectively, it could be said. "I would like to call Dr. Gerald Hanover to the stand."

"For what purpose?" Judge Hill asked.

"Dr. Hanover is a psychiatrist from St. Luke's Hospital here in Duluth," Art explained. "He is widely known and respected in the field of hypnotism. With the court's permission, we would like to conduct an experiment."

"A side show?" Judge Hill asked skeptically.

"No, your honor. But Dr. Hanover has examined Tom Garborg under hypnosis. We would like to repeat the procedure here."

"You don't object?" she asked Tom Garborg.

"No, your honor," Tom said boldly. "I have nothing to hide."

"Proceed," Judge Hill instructed.

After establishing Dr. Hanover's credentials and experience, he stepped down from the chair and Tom Garborg took the stand. Dr. Hanover gave Tom instructions on concentration, then said at the mention of the word "Runway" he would enter into a deep sleep; at the sound of the word "Airport" he would appear to awaken and that he would regain complete consciousness at the word "landing."

Tom's head dropped to his chest, his eyes closed. Dr. Hanover asked him several questions, to which there was no response. "You are now at the airport," Dr. Hanover said. Tom Garborg looked up, seemingly awake.

"It is Thursday afternoon, November second. Where are you?"

"Outside Bill and Hannah Crane's house," he said.

"What is happening?"

"They are all watching the house," he said.

"Who is?"

"Max, Rick and Dick," Tom said. "Oh, the dog is coming out."

"What is he doing?"

"He's running away. They are all following him. They're headed for the bank. No, the alley behind the bank. The dog has something in his mouth. He's running back to the Crane's house. They are all going after him. Oh, I hope they don't see me!"

Tom went on with a full description of the events of the day—detail by detail—until they got to the cabin.

"I'm out in back, looking in the window. That has to be Bill Crane lying there on the floor. There's blood all over the place. I'm going in to see if he is still alive."

"You don't know Bill Crane?" Dr. Hanover asked.

"No, I never met him," Tom said.

"Then why are you so interested in the kidnapping?"

"He ruined everything! He raped her! We had to come back from our honeymoon early."

"Your honeymoon?" Dr. Hanover asked.

"Yes," Tom said. "Carol sprained her ankle. Bad. She couldn't walk on it. We didn't know if it was broken or what. She spent the night at the hospital."

"And Bill Crane came to see her?"

"Yes. He told her he heard about her accident, so he wanted to come cheer her up. He tied a pillowcase around her mouth so she couldn't scream. Then he raped her! On our honeymoon! For God's sake, the man was an animal!"

Gasps went out from every corner of the room.

"Did Carol tell you about it right away?" Dr. Hanover asked.

"No," Tom said. "Not until she found out she was pregnant. We didn't know who the father of the baby was! That bastard! God, I hate him! I'll kill him if I get a chance. He makes me crazy! I can't even think straight! I don't know what I'm doing! Is he dead? God, I hope so."

"What did you do then?" Dr. Hanover asked.

"I...I don't know," Tom answered. No one could argue that it was the most sincere sounding answer they had ever heard. "I just know he made me go crazy. I don't know what to do. I want to kill him, but I can't! God, I'm a gutless failure! I can't even hurt the guy that did this to my wife!" He stopped, then let out a bloodcurdling cry.

"What is happening?" Dr. Hanover asked.

"I don't know. Everything is dark. So black. I can't see anything. I can't think. I don't know anything."

He paused again. "Why are they looking at me like that? Why is the dog licking my face? What am I doing out here in the woods by this tree? What happened?"

"You don't remember what happened?" Dr. Hanover asked.

****

"We have to get there in time," Ken Brown said as he pushed the gas pedal farther to the floorboard on his jeep. "Rick, if you can read my thoughts, hang on for a couple of minutes. We're almost there."

Alex Broquist sat beside him, clutching the dashboard with both hands until his knuckles turned white. Cock-A-Doodle-Doo was in his lap, his leash securely in place and wrapped around Alex's wrist. Alex didn't let go until Ken stopped the jeep in front of the courthouse. He hurried inside, Alex following after him.

"Rick!" Ken said to his son, placing his hand on his shoulder. "Can you come outside for a minute?"

"Dad!" Ken said, surprised by his appearance. He had vowed he wanted nothing to do with this whole mess. "What's wrong?"

"Nothing," he whispered. "Just come out into the hall."

Rick got up and followed his dad to where Alex was sitting.

"What's he doing here?" Rick asked. Everybody knew Alex Broquist only came into Willow Creek twice a year for supplies. He was an old trapper, living alone like a hermit in the woods. It would take a miracle for him to come to a big city like Duluth.

"He's got something to tell the judge," Ken said. "Just get in there and see if Art can get a couple of minutes to come out and hear his story."

"You are landing," Dr. Hanover said as Rick walked back into the courtroom. Tom Garborg snapped back to reality, unaware of what had happened while he had been *under*.

"Do you have any other witnesses?" Judge Hill asked.

"No, your honor," Art Moore said. "I believe..."

Rick walked up the aisle, went directly to Art, whispered something to him, then turned and walked back to his seat.

"If the court would allow," Art said, "I would like to request a brief recess. A witness may have come forward who saw exactly what happened at the scene of the crime."

Everyone was abuzz. Everybody from Willow Creek was already in the courtroom. Everyone except Ken Brown, and they all knew he had promised not to have anything to do with the whole trial. A witness?

"Granted," Judge Hill said, "you may have fifteen minutes. But this had better not be some trick."

"Thank you, your honor," Art said, then ran out into the hall.

"Come in here," he ordered Ken and Alex Broquist, who was pulling Cock-A-Doodle-Doo behind him, shooing them down to a conference room before anybody could see them.

****

"Are you sure?" he asked Alex after listening to his story.

"Of course I'm sure," Alex grumbled. "You think I'd come here if I wasn't sure? You know I hate the city!"

Art had to admit that Alex Broquist had to be the most credible witness anyone could ever ask for. It would take a major event for him to venture out of the woods, even to Willow Creek, much less to Duluth.

"And you will testify to this under oath?" Art asked him, not sure how he would react in front of all those people.

"The one thing my mother taught me was that you always tell the truth, no matter what it costs you," he said, walking towards the courtroom. "I'm ready."

****

"I would like to call Alex Broquist to the stand," Art said amidst an almost deafening rumble among the people who knew and recognized the "tree man," as everyone called Alex.

"You were at Bill Crane's cabin on the afternoon of November second?" Art asked Alex.

"I don't remember the date," Alex admitted, "but I heard a whole bunch of noise over there. I went over to see what was going on."

"Did anyone see you?" Art asked.

"I snuck around back so they wouldn't see me," Alex said. "I don't take much to people."

"So no one knew you were there?" Art asked.

"No," Alex repeated.

"What did you see?" Art asked.

"I looked in the window. I saw him..." Alex pointed to Tom Garborg.

"What was he doing?" Art asked.

"He was just standin' there. Watchin' the old man layin' there on the floor, bleedin' to death."

"Did he do anything?" Art questioned.

"Who, him?" Alex asked, again pointing to Tom.

"Yes," Art said.

"No," Alex said. "He just stood there. He looked real mad, but he didn't do nothin'."

"Then what did you see?"

"The old man, the one inside the cabin, he seemed to sort of come to a little bit. He must have heard all the commotion. So he grabbed his rifle. He must have saw somebody in the window, 'cuz he aimed right at it. He was all ready to fire a shot."

"Bill Crane was going to shoot Tom Garborg?" Art asked.

The courtroom went completely silent. A pin dropping would have echoed.

"That's what I said," Alex said. "Well, I couldn't just stand there and let him get killed. It wasn't right. I looked down, and like it was a miracle, there was a gun layin' on the ground. I picked it up and shot the old man to save that youngster's life. It was just a simple matter of tryin' to do what was right."

"But Bill Crane's gun wasn't loaded," Art said, playing the devil's advocate.

"I sure as anything didn't know that," Alex said. "I s'pect that Tom fellow didn't know it wasn't loaded, neither. And I'm sure as anything old Bill Crane didn't know there wasn't nothin' in the chamber."

"Thank you, Mr. Broquist," Art said. "Your honor, I would like to request that all charges against my client be dropped. It was clearly a case of self-defense."

The gavel fell heavily on the judge's desk, seeming to Tom Garborg to last forever. "Case dismissed!" Judge Hill announced. "Mr. Garborg, you are free to go."

As they all walked away, Rick turned back just in time to see Tom Garborg walk over to Alex Broquist and put his arm around his shoulders like they were old buddies. Alex grinned at him, shook his hand and said something too low for anyone to hear. They both laughed and climbed into Tom's car. They waved at Rick and Max as they drove past them.

"Strange friendship," Rick commented.

Max looked at them and shook her head. "Yeah, real strange. Wonder what that's all about?"

And the odd twosome disappeared down the road that would take Alex back to his little tarpaper shack and his solitude. Soon Tom would be heading back to Minneapolis and Carol and Michael and a new baby. Life would be back to normal, with one exception: Bill Crane would never bother another woman again.

As Alex got out of Tom's car, he grinned toothlessly, waved goodbye and said, "All's well that ends well. Nobody will ever know we had it all figgered out ahead of time."

"You got it," Tom said as he drove away. His cell phone rang, and he reached for it instinctively.

"Tom?" Carol's mother said. "You'd better hurry if you want to see your baby born."

The tires squealed as he shifted into high gear and sped down the road. Yeah, he decided. It ended real well. One life was gone. One good-for-nothing low-life. But another new one—an innocent, sweet one—was about to begin. It was worth it. They had done what so many people had tried to do: they got away with murder.

A LETTER FROM THE AUTHOR

More and more, people are moving from the big cities to rural areas and small towns. At the same time, young people who venture out on their own into the big, wild world discover that life isn't as easy as they thought it would be. These "adult children" are making their way back home to their parents, the very thing they vowed they would never do.

What makes life in small towns different from that in the big city? Primarily, the people. You can live in a city and never know your next-door neighbor. In the country's small towns, everybody knows everybody's business, and usually tries to make it their own business as well.

I lived in a very small town in northern Minnesota from the time I was in the seventh grade until I graduated from high school. The little town was Spring Lake, with "a population of 50, if you count the dogs and cats," as my dad used to say. High school for me was in Deer River, MN, with a population of a whopping 600 at that time. While none of the people in *Bank Roll* are real people, I have to admit that the people I knew in Deer River were "real characters." If any of the residents of Deer River think they recognize some of the characters who are friends of Max Stryker, I will argue that they are all purely fictional characters, and any resemblance to real people is completely coincidental. Meanwhile, I truly loved life in Deer River, as well as its residents. They say you can't go home, but in a way, I feel like I have done just that in spending time with Max Stryker in her home in Willow Creek.

I want to make mention, too, of a very special young person. I met his mother, Joyce Anthony, in some online groups where we are both members. We "clicked" instantly, and I got acquainted with her son, Shane D. Foster, through her. Shane is a wonderfully talented young man, who has just entered that scary world of teenagerdom. He created the cover art for *Bank Roll*. I owe a huge debt of gratitude to Shane for his input in this book, as well as that of his art instructor, Paul Deniro, who supervised and inspired Shane.

And just to prove that life is indeed often stranger than fiction, I wrote *Bank Roll* nearly five years before it was published. I had put it away and pretty much forgotten about it. In February, 2006, I decided that since it was all finished, I might as well see about having it published. Max Stryker, in the book, worked for the St. Paul, MN newspaper, *Pioneer Press*. She lost her job. Just a few days after I finished the final edit on it, the news all across the nation spread that Knight Ridder, the parent company of the *Pioneer Press,* had been sold. In less than 24 hours, the *Pioneer Press* was being put up for sale, apparently an unwanted child to the new owners. If Max Stryker were working at the *Pioneer Press* in March, 2006, she might well have been handed the pink slip she was toying with as *Bank Roll* opens and headed back to Willow Creek.

I love to hear from readers. You can reach me at janetelainesmith@yahoo.com or find more about me and my books at http://www.janetelainesmith.com or write me at P.O. Box 126, East Grand Forks, MN 56721. And stay tuned, because Max Stryker won't stay out of trouble forever. This is just the start of something good. The next Max Stryker Mystery will be *Lights Out*.

READERS GROUP GUIDE

1. Have you ever lived in both a small town and a big city? What was the biggest difference to you?
2. Have you had an "adult child" come home, or have you been one yourself who was forced to return to your parents' home?
3. Did Max Stryker have any business sticking her nose in police business when she wasn't properly trained to be in the way of danger?
4. Could you sympathize with Rick Brown in the loss of his mother?
5. Did it seem odd for Rick to help Max, considering his feelings about police business?
6. Did you think Sally and Paul Bunyan might have been guilty of the kidnapping?
7. What did you think of the FBI and their role in the case?
8. Do you think Max should have kept on with the case after Pops had his heart attack, or should she have insisted on going to the hospital?
9. Who was your favorite character, and why?
10. Do you think Hannah Crane was justified in her actions?
11. Do you think Bill Crane should have been killed, or would the book have been just as good if he had survived?
12. Is it possible for some people to get away with murder without getting caught? (I call it my O.J. Simpson Syndrome!)

Printed in the United States
100315LV00005B/262/A

NORMANDALE COMMUNITY COLLEGE
LIBRARY
9700 FRANCE AVENUE SOUTH
BLOOMINGTON, MN 55431-4399